A MOST DEMANDING CUSTOMER...

Jake, the guitar player at Callahan's Place, felt the universe spinning around him as the presence of the evil Beast, who had traveled across space to enslave Callahan's resident alien Mickey Finn, came closer and closer.

"I have nearly reached you now. Soon I will be physically present, and able to restart the slave Finn," the Beast said telepathically.

"He'll find a way to beat you. He won't let his wife down!" Jake protested.

"I will promise him that if he . . . fights my war for me, I will revive his people, and give them a planet to use as they wish. This one will do admirably . . ."

> "Robinson is the hottest writer to hit science fiction since Ellison, and he can match the master's frenetic energy and emotional intensity, arm-break for gut-wrench."
>
> —*Los Angeles Times*

Berkley Books by Spider Robinson

CALLAHAN'S CROSSTIME SALOON
MINDKILLER
NIGHT OF POWER
CALLAHAN'S SECRET

SPIDER ROBINSON

CALLAHAN'S SECRET

BERKLEY BOOKS, NEW YORK

All the stories in this volume previously appeared in *Analog Science Fact/Science Fiction* magazine; copyrights have been reassigned to the author by Davis Publications.

CALLAHAN'S SECRET

A Berkley Book / published by arrangement with
the author

PRINTING HISTORY
Berkley edition / July 1986
Second printing / August 1986
Third printing / December 1986

ISBN: 0-425-10059-6

A BERKLEY BOOK ® TM 757,375
Berkley Books are published by The Berkley Publishing Group,
200 Madison Avenue, New York, NY 10016.
The name "BERKLEY" and the stylized "B" with design
are trademarks belonging to Berkley Publishing Corporation.

PRINTED IN THE UNITED STATES OF AMERICA

For Eleanor Wood,
and Susan Allison

TABLE OF CONTENTS

FOREWORD

There's something we have to get absolutely clear right at the outset, and if you think you detect a dangerous gleam in my eye, you are perfectly right.

Ordinarily I am rather a hard man to insult. This is partly because I am blessed with a self-confidence so pervasive that it is frequently mistaken for smugness by less fortunate souls, and partly because I am abnormally lazy even for a writer—if you're insulted, you're supposed to *do* something about it, so I usually decline to take offence even when offered some.

I'm especially hard to insult professionally, as I am willing to shamelessly admit, having practiced many of the most disgusting and heinous vices in literature—I freely confess here and now that in the twelve years since I gave up honest work I have committed editorship (twice!), agentry (also twice), and book reviewing (multiple counts), and at least one grand jury is still considering allegations of literary criticism which I have given up denying.

To my own mild surprise, however, I discover that I do have some small shreds of literary pride left, and I wish to preserve them . . . so there's something we've got to get straight. No kidding around, now, God damn it; I'm serious. Pay attention:

Yes, this is a book of stories set in the tavern known as Callahan's Place.

Yes, it is the last such book.

Yes, there were others.

Okay, there were two such others.

All right, dammit, yes, Berkley *is* packaging all of them as a unit, with coordinated covers and so forth.

Nevertheless and notwithstanding, and we'd better be straight on this or there's gonna be blood in the scuppers: *I have **not** written a trilogy.*

Repeat: not. It just so happens, by chemically pure chance, that this series of stories has reached its conclusion coincidental with the completion of the volume immediately following the one that succeeded the first one. That does *not* make it a trilogy.

In the first place it is not booby-trapped like most trilogies are. Neither of those first two volumes ended in the middle of a story, leaving you in midair in plot terms (although the first one, admittedly, did leave Mike Callahan literally in midair). If you have never read a Callahan's Place book before, you should find this as good a place to start as any: since these yarns were designed for magazine publication, each is self-contained, and you should feel no need for any wordy What-Has-Gone-Before synopsis. If you have the first book but missed the second, it won't cripple your appreciation of this one. If you feel you *want* to own all three volumes, who am I to tell you what to do with your money?—but I didn't plan this whole thing to sucker you into laying out extra dollars, like Chico Marx with his "tootsie-frootsie ice-a cream" routine.

In the second place, it was not *my* idea to end this series or cycle or saga or whatever you want to call it (and I don't care what you call it as long as you don't call it a trilogy). That was done for me, by events beyond my control, and believe me, nobody is sadder about it than I am—no, not even my publishers, my editor, my agent, the people who currently own the TV and film options, or my more substantial creditors, all of whom have been heard to express dismay.

Of course it's a financial disaster for me, but I don't care about that. (I also don't much mind having red-hot bobby-pins rammed up underneath my fingernails.) It's a professional disaster as well, since now I'll have to think up *all* my own plots rather than simply dramatizing the yarns that Jake tells me—but after all, I have published seven books in which Callahan's Place is never mentioned, so the increased creative demand shouldn't prove too arduous. (I'll simply give up eating on days ending in "y".) There's even a vague feeling of something like relief in leaving the nest of Callahan's and going out into the world to make my own way; twelve years is a long time to spend in any bar.

And still a part of me wishes fervently that it didn't have to end this way.

I'm going to miss Mike a *lot*.

Association with Callahan's Place has certainly made life interesting this past dozen years—and usually pleasantly so. It got me out of the sewer, for one thing (see the Foreword to CALLAHAN'S CROSSTIME SALOON). It has made me a great many friends I might not otherwise have met, and one or two enemies I'd have acquired sooner or later anyway. And it has been responsible for some memorable moments. (Catch me at a convention sometime, and ask me about the reader who invited me aboard his nuclear submarine—or the one who called at 5 A.M. threatening to commit suicide if I didn't tell him how to get to Callahan's, *right now.*)

But fate has taken a hand, as they say, and the Callahan's Place saga/series/cycle (just don't use that "t" word) seems to have reached its conclusion with this volume.

Does that mean, necessarily, that it has reached its completion? Will there never be another story set in that splendid fiction?

Well, in a way, from a certain perspective, I hope so. I know I've always been rather glad that Giovanni Guareschi stopped writing about Don Camillo when he did, and the recent explosion of tourism has ruined the planet Arrakis for me forever. You can work a good thing to death, and beyond. It may be time for Callahan's Place to tumble over the Reichenbach Falls . . .

On the other hand, I'm certain that there are Callahan's

Place stories Jake has never told me, things that happened in the past that he hasn't gotten around to reporting—he hints at a couple in the pages that follow. Right now, however, for reasons that will probably become clear before you've finished this book, he doesn't much want to talk about Callahan's—and besides, for reasons that should also shortly become clear, he's too busy. But I'm at least intuitively certain that there are still a few stories he could tell if he felt like it.

Just don't look to see them any time soon—if ever.

Last thoughts, before I go:

In the final chapter of this book, Jake reveals more than one "Callahan's Secret." One of them—you'll know it when you get to it—is, rather literally, I'm afraid, potential dynamite. Consequently I must ask you to keep the secret, and above all to try and ensure that your copy of this book does *not* fall into the hands of anyone above the rank of corporal in any military establishment on Earth. Perhaps I should have suppressed the story altogether. But I've been sleeping a lot easier since Jake told *me*, and so I'm going to take a chance and trust you. We should be safe—if anyone in military planning circles read science fiction, we probably wouldn't all have gotten into this fix in the first place. But keep it to yourself, okay?

And remember: no matter what anybody says, this is NOT a trilogy...

So long, Michael. It's been a privilege to know you. Thanks for the laughs. And, come to think of it, for the tears, too. "Shared pain is diminished; shared joy is increased"—you taught me that a long time ago.

I'll miss you, I will.

Halifax,
April 8, 1985

CALLAHAN'S SECRET

CHAPTER 1

The Blacksmith's Tale

ONCE I BOUGHT a watch whose battery was rated for one year. The next time I gave it a thought was when it failed—four years later. Something familiar cannot be odd, until it stops.

Similarly, there is no set opening time at Callahan's Place. Once I came by at three in the afternoon, to talk to Callahan about something, and found that the place had been open for over an hour; another time I arrived at 7 P.M. and Mike was just opening the door. But somehow, for the better part of a decade, it never struck me that the Place was always open when I arrived—until the night it wasn't.

Nearly nine o'clock of a warm wet summer evening, and the door was shut tight. Only dim light came through the windows, nothing like the warm cheery glow the Place has when it's open, and the only thing in the parking lot besides my own car was a big beat-up van I didn't recognize.

The rain complicated things. I don't mind rain a lot, and I *like* it when it's warm—as it was that night—but it had been coming down hard for the last fifteen minutes, and so the note posted on the door was only partly legible. I could translate *"empor rily losed f r enovat ons,"* and *"doo pens at,"* but the *time* at which the doo' would 'pen was three blurs, all rounded at the top. Perhaps "9:00," perhaps "9:20" or "9:30." Or perhaps it read "8:30," and the job, whatever it was, was running overtime. Worst, there was a big long blur *after* the time. It might have said "9:00 sharp," but it could just as easily have been "3:00 Friday."

When that watch battery I mentioned earlier finally failed,

1

I buried it in my backyard, respectful of its magnificent achievement. But that was after reflection. My first reaction was acute annoyance. I thought my watch had failed me.

So it was now. I could think of several ways to go kill some time—but how much time? Meanwhile I was getting soaked. So I did what I don't think I would have done under other circumstances.

I opened the door and walked in.

I knew it wouldn't be locked, because there is no lock on that door. In the dozen years I've been coming to Callahan's, there've been four attempted afterhours burglaries that I know of. None of them used the front door; none bothered to try. (Callahan dealt with them situationally. One is now a regular customer, and never mind which one; another, a hard-guy type, got two broken elbows.)

But I should have knocked first, and waited for Mike to open the door or holler "Come in," and gone away if he didn't.

Which he wouldn't have—there was no sign of him when I had closed the door behind me. But I failed to notice; once I'd wiped my glasses dry, I was too busy being thunderstruck.

Do you remember that time I told you about once, when I walked into Callahan's to find a mirror behind the bar, where no mirror had ever been before? And it disoriented me so much that I mistook my reflection for an approaching demon, with "horns" that were really the brim of my Stetson hat? This was like that. Something as familiar as Callahan's Place is not supposed to change. The watch battery is supposed to last forever. I may have actually twitched and squeaked, I don't know.

The light was as bad as it had been that other time, with the mirror, and so once again my brain, trying to resolve unexpected data into a pattern, made a first approximation that vaguely matched something in its files and served me up a trial hallucination. For a predator such as man, a wrong guess can be preferable to a slow one.

What I thought I saw, off to my left, a few yards away,

was a *giant* ebony snake, maybe three feet in diameter, coiled around a tree, scales shimmering in the semidarkness. Tree and snake appeared to extend up through the ceiling without rupturing it.

I blinked and it wasn't a snake, it was an immense DNA double helix clinging to a barber pole, pulsing dully with life. So I blinked again.

(First the predator brain searches the file of Dangerous Things. If that doesn't work, it tries Nondangerous Living Things. Only then does it calm down and search all the other files. Two seconds, tops.)

It was a spiral staircase up to the roof.

"Cushla machree," I said softly.

What had made it seem to be a *double* helix was the heavy railing which paralleled the stairs. The "scales" were the spaces between the railing supports. The apparent shimmering and/or pulsing was because one of the very few lights in the room, a small flourescent behind the bar, was flickering rapidly.

I said (prophetically enough) that I would be. dipped in shit, but I relaxed. I was beginning to understand.

Mike Callahan lets his customers take their drinks up on the roof if the weather's agreeable. There's a dumbwaiter to ferry cash down and drinks up. But until now the only access for humans and most other customers had been a vertical ladder and hatch. Some of the regulars had trouble getting up the ladder due to age or infirmity. Certain others could get *up* just fine—but found that the added ballast of four or five drinks seriously disrupted their balance on the way *down*. Something about the center of gravity shifting, Doc Webster said. Just a few days before, Shorty Steinitz had broken an ankle—and here was Callahan's response.

"Hey, Mike," I called out, and got no answer. The curtain behind the bar was closed. I had gall enough to enter Callahan's bar uninvited, but not his living space. I called his name once more and wandered over to inspect the new staircase.

It was a cast iron joy to behold. I'm totally ignorant

about such things, but I could tell that it was *old,* and *beautiful,* and very well designed. You could not fall down that staircase. You couldn't even bark your shin. It was so well installed that it looked like it'd been there for years—except for the odd bits of welding spatter in the sawdust on the floor—and indeed it fit right in with the atmosphere of Callahan's Place. Ornamented rather than starkly functional, subtly and ingeniously worked in ways I was not competent to appreciate even if the light had been adequate, it would not have looked out of place in a cellar jazz joint or a monastery, might have done time in both. It invited one to climb it.

So I did.

The footing was secure, the risers precisely the right height, the treads precisely the right depth. It had to be a modular assembly. A single giant staircase, even if it had happened to fit through the front door, would have required trucks, cranes, dollies, rollers, block and tackle and much time—whereas an assembly job this size could conceivably have been installed in a single day by two or three big skilled men. But it was so *cunningly* assembled that it was hard to be sure. This had to have cost Callahan a bundle.

I wound my way around and up until I stood in a sort of hut with a door opening onto the roof. I thought about rainwater spilling down into the bar below, but when I experimentally opened the door a crack, there was no flood. I pushed it open and the everpresent sound of rain went from bass rumble to treble hiss. It seemed to be easing up.

The rain did not spill indoors because the floor of the hut was slightly higher than the roof. But you did not have to remember to step down; there was a short ramp. I know little more about carpentry than I do about iron work—but I know good design when I fail to trip over it. It figured that Mike Callahan would hire the best man available to do surgery on his Place.

The door closed quickly; some unseen damping mechanism kept it from slamming; in the rain it made no sound at all. I walked around the hut once, admiring it . . . then walked around it again, admiring the countryside.

I'm sure you know the strange, special magic of high places. Have you ever been on one at night? In the warm rain?

To be sure, Callahan's roof is a wonderful place from which to view the world in nearly any weather. The land falls sharply away to the north and east, and incredibly for Long Island (even for Suffolk County) it is largely undeveloped, raw trees as far as you can make out. To the south and west, beyond the parking lot, runs Route 25A, sparsely lined with garishly lit sucker traps. (Fairly heavy traffic, but Callahan doesn't get a lot of transient trade. The parking lot is hid by tall hedges, the driveway is inconspicuous; the only sign is the one over the front door.) Beyond the highway you can just make out one of the more expensive subdivisions, well zoned, landscaped and cared for; on Christmas Eve, with a couple of Irish coffees warming your belly and all the lights blazing in the distance, it looks . . . well, Christmasy.

Tonight the roof was a warm flat rock on which many large somethings were peeing, from a great height. The highway looked glorious—people who wear glasses are lucky, we have stars on rainy nights—but my clothes were getting wet. Wetter. I considered ducking back inside . . . but as I said, I *like* warm rain. I particularly like to be naked in warm rain, and don't get a lot of opportunities. Mike wouldn't mind, and anyone else I would see drive up.

So I stripped and looked about for the driest place to stash my clothes.

The dumbwaiter seemed like the best bet; I could wedge its door open with something to keep it up here at roof level. I padded barefoot toward its tall housing—and discovered that it was already so wedged, with a chisel. Inside was a pile of clothing. Big man's clothes, faded jeans, denim shirt, boots, sized to fit only one man I knew. That solved the mystery of Callahan's whereabouts. He must be a secret naked-in-the-rain nut, too. He was going to jump a foot in the air when I came around the dumbwaiter. This would be good for laughs—and it might cost him a couple of drinks to keep the story to myself...

It was just possible that my fellow nudist was not Callahan—in which case I was properly dressed to meet him. Onward.

I should have *lifted up* the jeans. The underwear might have warned me. I piled my clothes on top of the others, walked around the dumbwaiter, and became one myself. Waiting, dumb, one foot in the air. She was very beautiful, and in the instant I saw her I wanted urgently to *do this right,* to not make any mistakes. It was not going to be easy.

I am sorry to say that you would probably not have thought she was beautiful—unless you, too, are a pervert. I mean, going naked in the rain is one thing, but I'm talking major league perversion here. (From my point of view, I am the only sane man in a perverted culture. Perverts always feel that way.)

I will state the perversion: I like women who look like women. That is, my ideal of feminine beauty adheres closely to that which has been the generally accepted consensus from the dawn of time until quite recently and quite locally.

What you would probably have said if you'd seen her, naked or clothed, is, "Handsome woman; she could be beautiful if she lost the weight." You would probably have gallantly tried to avoid looking at, let alone commenting on her body—you almost certainly would not have drunk the sight of it the way I did.

She did not, in other words, look the way North America thinks women should look. She did not look like a thirteen-year-old boy with plums in his shirt pockets. Those were her clothes in the dumbwaiter. And I do not even mean that she was a Jayne Mansfield/Loni Anderson type, with one of those big bodies that seem packed tight, compressed snugly by invisible plastic, firm as a weightlifter's shoulder. She had big glorious saggy tits, and what are sometimes affectionately called "love handles," (that is, the people who use the term sometimes mean it affectionately) and a round belly and thighs that would jiggle when she walked.

She looked, in short, much like half the mature women in this sorry culture, and she would have opened the nose of most of the heterosexual males who ever lived. Praxiteles, Titian, Rubens, Rodin, any of the great ones would have reached for their tools, if not their work utensils, at the sight of her.

You know: a whale. A hippo. I'm telling ya, Morty, this broad was a hunnert'eighty, hun'ninety pounds if she was a friggin' ounce, no shit. One of America's millions of rejects, forever barred from The Good Life, too sunk in sloth or genetic degeneracy to torture herself into the semblance of an undernourished adolescent male. A pig. No character, no willpower, no self-discipline, no self-respect, certainly no sex appeal. A lifelong figure of fun, doomed to be jolly, member of the only minority group that "comedians" like Joan Rivers can still get away with viciously assaulting.

I could tell I was beginning to get an erection.

So I used the second I had left to study her face. A socially difficult moment was imminent, and I wanted it to go well, so I needed to know as much about her as possible, immediately.

Big lush women and small slight men in our society go through life wrapped around a softball-sized chunk of pain; it breaks some of them and makes others magnificent. She was magnificent. Clearly visible on her face, written plain for any fool to see, were the character, will power, self-discipline, self-respect and warm sexiness which common wisdom said she could not possibly have without automatically becoming skinny. She had lots of laugher's wrinkles and a couple of thinker's wrinkles and no other kinds. She wore her hair in a big bush of curls that made no futile attempt to downplay her size; rain-sparkle made it a halo. The split-second glance I got of her eyes, glistening in the light from the all-night deli across the road, focused on the far distance, made them seem serene, self-confident.

I went on computer time. And a very good computer it must have been, too, because I was able to run several very complex subprograms in the second or so allotted to me. One routine sorted through the several hundred thousand Opening Lines in storage for something suitable to Unexpected Encounter With Nude Stranger, but since it expected to come up empty, a more ambitious program attempted to create something new, something witty and engaging and reassuring, out of the materials of the situation. In hopes that one or the other would succeed, a simple and well-used program began selecting the tone and pitch of voice and the manner of delivery—soft enough not to startle, but not so soft as to seem wimpy; humorous but not clownish; urbane but not smug; admiring but not lecherous—prepared, in short, to begin lying through its/my teeth. Meanwhile, an almost unconscious algorithm had me keep my hands firmly at my sides and stand up a little straighter. And all of this together took up, at most, 20 percent of the available bytes—the rest was fully occupied in an urgent priority task.

Memorizing her...

Plenty of time! Computational capacity to spare! I knew that she was beginning to become aware of me several hundred nanoseconds before she did, integrated all the subprograms, picked a neutral Opening Line and pinned my hopes on delivery, ran a hundred full dress rehearsals to derive best- and worst-case results, made the go decision, and had time to admire her lower left eyelash and myself before I heard my very own voice say, with all the warmth and tone and clarity I could reasonably have hoped for, "It certainly is a very nice tits."

My central processing unit melted down into slag.

It took her ten years to turn and look at me, and no thought of any kind took place inside my skull; horror fused every circuit. She looked me square in the eye, absolutely expressionlessly, for endless decades, while I marinated in failure and shame. Then her gaze left my eyes, panned slowly downward. It rested on my mouth for many years, moved on down again, did not pause until it reached my feet, then came back up again and paused where it was bound to eventually—but I was centuries dead by then, only a cinder of consciousness remained in my brain to be snuffed by the realization that my erection was now up to at least half mast, and so by the time her gaze got back up to my eyes, I don't see how she could possibly have seen glowing therefrom the slightest light of intelligence.

The animal who sleeps under my computer woke up and tried its best. It tried for a smile, doubtless produced a horrible grimace. It essayed a merry laugh, managed to generate a hideous gargling sound. It gestured vaguely, attempting a Gallic shrug and failing to bring it off. To all of this she displayed no visible reaction whatever. The old animal gave up.

The first plan I formed was to jump off the roof, but the problem with that was that it could only be done once and might not hurt enough long enough, so I stepped closer to the dumbwaiter housing and began battering my head against it to soften my skull up for the grand finale, and I liked the way it felt and began to get a rhythm going, and then and only then did she burst out into a magnificent bellow of laughter, a great trombone hoot of shocked merriment, and big as she was she was up out of tailor's seat and holding me away from the dumbwaiter before I could deliver it another blow, and then there was a great complicated rocking struggling hugging stumbling confusion of laughter and tears and rain that somehow left us sitting on our asses on that wet roof with our feet touching, both of us shuddering with mirth. We nearly got our breath back a few minutes later, but when she tried to speak all she got out was "smooth" before dissolving into hysterics again, and a little after that I managed to get out, "My Freudian slip is—" before I lost it, and when the earthquake had well and truly passed I was lying flat on my back with rain running up my nostrils and the soles of my feet pressed firmly against human warmth. My hands hurt a little from beating them on the roof.

I sat up.

So did she. I must have looked forlorn. My erection was gone. "It's okay," she said, pressing her toes gently against mine. "I've heard worse."

"You don't understand," I moaned.

"Admittedly—but I think I got the message."

"But—"

"It was, unquestionably, the most memorable meeting of my life, and nothing will ever top it." Oh, if only she'd been right.

I was beginning slowly to realize that this situation was salvageable—that the disaster was of such epic proportion as to be a kind of triumph. I had certainly made an impression on her. Was this not Callahan's Place—albeit empty—beneath my butt? Callahan's Place, focus of strange and wonderful events, magical tavern in which nothing was impossible and few things even unlikely? Could there be any better, more fitting place for a miracle to happen than here on Callahan's roof?

But exactly where to go from here was hidden from me. "I'm Jake."

"I'm glad. I thought you might have really hurt yourself there."

"I meant that my name is Jake."

"Glad to hear it. What *is* your name?"

Better and better. I like them quick. "Damned if I know. What's yours? And *please* don't say, 'Thanks, I'll have a beer.'"

"I'm Mary, Jake."

With what feeble wits I had left, I attempted a cunning investigation. "You must know the guys who put in that splendid staircase, right?"

She went two degrees cooler. "I put in the staircase."

"Excuse me," I said faintly, and got to my feet. The dumbwaiter housing felt just as good as it had before; there was just enough give to it to cause an energetic rebound, but not so much as to soften the impact.

Unexpectedly my ears hurt, and the rhythm of my head was halted. *"Stop that,"* she said, twisting me by both ears to face her. "Damn it, I had no business getting chilly at you that way. I must be the first lady blacksmith you've ever run into, how the hell could you know? You did good: you didn't look disbelieving, just surprised."

I shook my head. It stayed on. "You're the *second* woman smith I've met. That's why I'm mad at myself—I should have guessed."

She stepped back a pace and put her hands on her hips. "Jake," she said softly, "you're trying too hard."

"I know. Is it flattering at least?"

Her laugh was a good hearty bray. "Yes, by damn. And not entirely ineffective: I can't wait to find out what you're like when you're normal."

I felt my breathing begin to slow and my shoulders begin to relax. "I've always wondered myself. But at my worst I should have known that you put in that staircase."

"Why?"

"Because you *look* like the person who did it. Everything it takes to do a job that good, you've got, I could see that before you knew I was here, so I should have figured it out."

She dimpled. "There, you see? You finally got a compliment out straight—you're getting better."

"Where did it come from?"

"It spent its early years in the library of a wealthy bishop. For the last thirty years it was in the best whorehouse in Brooklyn, but the place closed down a few months back—"

I was stricken. "Lady Sally's is *closed?*"

She nodded sadly. "Too much cutrate competition. Changing fashions. Nowadays they all seem to want sleaze, and a place like Sally's is out of style."

"My God! I *know* that staircase! Do you mean to tell me that *Lady Sally McGee's staircase is here in Callahan's bar?*" I began to smile through my sorrow. "Ah, God, Sally," I said to the weeping heavens, "I'm sorry they closed you down, the world is a darker place—but at least all your treasures haven't fallen among heathens. Mary, where is the grand old lady, do you know?"

"Enjoying her retirement. This is a good home for the staircase, then?"

"Only the very best. This is *Callahan's Place,* do you see? No, how could you see?"

"The way you could see that I was a good smith, maybe. There *is* something about the place. But I—"

"Be sure. If the staircase had legs, it would have walked here. Miracles happen here—a little like the ones that happened at Lady Sally's, come to think. Is Mike planning to open tonight, do you know?"

"About half an hour from now, he said."

"Then you'll see. You'll like the gang—they're the best family I ever had. Did Mike tell you about the house rules?"

"House rules?"

"Every drink in the house costs half a buck. Mike accepts nothing but singles. On your way out you collect whatever change you have coming from the cigar-box full of quarters on the end of the bar—unless you've been visiting the fireplace—"

"Hold it. The drinks are half a buck?"

"Yeah, why?"

"These days a *beer* in most bars costs more than a dollar."

"Really? I don't go to any other bars."

"And nobody rips off the quarters? He must watch the box like a hawk—"

"Nope. Nobody watches the box. That's some of what I mean about Callahan's Place."

She shook her head gently. "Go on. Something about 'visiting the fireplace'—"

"If you feel the urge to, or the need to, you step up to the chalk line and face the fireplace. You have to make a toast aloud, and everyone shuts up while you do. Then you deep-six your glass, into the fireplace. It costs you your change for that drink, but it can really take a load off your shoulders sometimes."

"My," she said softly.

"People tend to come here when they're in need of help,

not always but pretty often. They get it, most times. We help each other. These days, it's getting hard to find a bar where the bartender'll even pretend to listen to your troubles anymore. At Callahan's Place *everybody* will listen to your problems. Respectfully. Carefully. You can't imagine the stories that get told here, sometimes."

"Sounds like a depressing place to get drunk."

I grinned. "You'll see. Everyone else must have come by earlier and seen that sign down on the front door before it got rained on, they'll be here soon. A merry crew, one and all. I give you fair warning: we are all paronomasiacs."

Her eyes widened in horror. "God, no! Not *punsters!*"

"But it's all right—tonight isn't Punday."

"Punday."

"The night on which the worst punster gets his or her tab refunded."

She staggered. "Christ, that was close. Too close."

"No, tonight is Tall Tales Night—and I'll tell you, it takes a lot to qualify as a tall tale in Callahan's. We've had a real talking dog, for instance. And a whole slew of time travelers. Two aliens... Say, there's one of them now." I waved. *"Hi, Finn!"*

She turned and saw him, and stood very still.

Well, how *could* I have prepared her? Callahan's Place is like that, you have to sink or swim. It was her turn.

Mickey Finn had been decelerating sharply when I first caught sight of him; he came in the last hundred yards like a seagull and landed with much more grace. Rain declined to fall on him—one reason I'd spotted him in the darkness—and when he was standing beside us the rain ignored us too. "Hello, Jake my friend." He politely began to undress.

"Not necessary, Mickey. Real good to see you, man— it's been too long! Allow me to present Mary. Mary, this is my friend Mickey Finn."

Mary was transfixed. That surprised me. This woman had not been visibly fazed by encountering a naked stranger of the opposite sex, while herself naked, in a remote place;

I had expected her to take Finn more or less in stride. I will admit that, considered dispassionately, a naked man *is* less startling than a flying man, particularly a flying man who stands six-eleven-and-a-half, has a magnificent craggy face and eyes like oxyacetylene blowtorches, and repels moisture. But *I* was the naked man in question. I found myself mildly irritated.

Still, if Mary was having difficulty rising to this social challenge, the gallant thing to do was to help. Finn was visibly wondering if he should offer his hand, so I offered him mine. After a genuinely warm handshake—I like the big cyborg—I gently tugged his hand in the direction of the new stairwell. "Mary put in the staircase over there. You ought to check it out, it's *special*." I winked with the eye Mary couldn't see. "Why don't you see if you can find Callahan while you're down there, see about getting this joint opened up for the night?"

Finn surprised me, too, a little—by taking his cue smoothly and without hesitation. He gets more sophisticated in human ways (excuse me, in Terran ways) every time I see him. "Certainly, Jake. We'll talk when you come down. It was very nice meeting you, Mary." He left quickly on those long legs, and even after the stairwell door had closed behind him, the rain kept failing to land on us. I would have loved to spend an hour trying to figure out how Finn did that—before asking him—but I was busy.

Mary was still standing exactly as she had been when Finn first landed, pivoted slightly to her left, looking even further left, smack through the spot where Finn had been. She hadn't moved a muscle.

I cleared my throat.

"Aliens, okay," she said in a clear, calm voice, still not moving, "but I don't believe you've had a talking dog."

I took it as a sign of recovery. "We didn't either, at first. Fella came in trying to cadge drinks with the old talking dog routine. Of course, we figured it was a ventriloquism scam—and so it was. The guy was a mute, and the dog was a mutant—*he was the ventriloquist*. They partnered up because they were lonely—nobody would talk to either of them, alone. They hang out here a lot, now."

She straightened from her pivot, worked her shoulders slightly, then relaxed. "He certainly is."

"Who certainly is what?"

"He certainly is a Mickey Finn."

She still wasn't entirely back in the world. But the part that was, was out of this world. Now that she was rainproof, droplets hung all over her body like facets on a precious stone, some standing still, some, like my gaze, trying to migrate downward. I wrestled my gaze up as high as I could manage, and thought of something that might reach her. "Those certainly are a very nice night."

It worked. It took her a second to get it, and then she laughed, about Force Six. "Jake," she said, "you've got a nice-looking evening yourself. I think I'm going to like this bar. Do you suppose this no-rain gimmick would work on our clothes if we took them out and put them on? Or is it necessary to dress before going downstairs?"

"Not necessary, no, but clothes *are* customarily worn. But don't ask me how Finn's technology works—the only way to find out is to try."

Sure enough, the rain avoided our clothing, too. "Of course," I said, "they'll get wet when we put them—" and then stopped. I wasn't wet any more. Neither was she. Our *hair* was dry, and I hadn't felt a breeze. My own clothes, which had been damp when I left them, were dry, and stayed that way.

"Fascinating," she murmured, for all the world like Mr. Spock.

I nodded. "Finn's great to have around in winter." I tossed her clothes to her, and she caught the stack. I began dressing myself. Do you think it silly that after having spent considerable time naked together, we averted our eyes as we dressed? I'm sure we both thought so—but we did it.

I liked her just as well, dressed. That is to say: dressed, she made me want to see her undressed again, as soon as possible. I wished the light was better. I could faintly hear sounds from below us, distant thuds and voices, one of them unmistakably Callahan's. Doc Webster's Studebaker pulled into the parking lot, followed by Long-Drink McGonnigle's truck, and way off down 25A I could hear Fast Eddie's Hideousmobile approaching. Callahan's Place was getting ready for a late opening.

She gestured vaguely at the weepy heavens above (and I couldn't help wondering how the raindrops knew enough not to fall in the path of her moving arm) and said, "Finn's from . . . well, out there, isn't he?"

"Yep. *Way* out."

"How long has he been here?"

"A little over ten years now, I make it."

"And he's spent the whole time hanging out in bars? What the hell was his mission?"

"The extermination of human life."

"Dammit, Jake, that's not funny."

"Don't panic—he defected. A long time ago, a couple of weeks after he arrived. His first night at Callahan's Place."

She visibly relaxed, but her face had a funny expression. "I see. Say no more, by all means. I think you've certainly covered all the high points of the story."

So I told her all about Finn, about the night he came to Callahan's and acquired his name—*just* in the nick of time.* I told her about the night he took on Adolph Hitler out in the parking lot, and how big the resulting crater was, until he fixed it. I told her about his successive careers as a farmer, a fisherman, a forest fire-watcher, and a lighthousekeeper, and by then I got the idea that I was talking entirely too much about Finn and decided to try for a smooth segue to some more rewarding topic.

"But enough about Finn. Let's talk about me. I am, in no particular order, a singer, a songwriter, a guitar player, a nice person, and in no particular order. I play here some nights with Fast Eddie the piano player, and we're very good. I have many of my original teeth and no ex-wives or children living and I find you the most devastatingly at-

*see "The Guy With The Eyes," CALLAHAN'S CROSSTIME SALOON. (Berkley) tractive woman I've met in at least a decade: I would *very* much like to know you better."

"Are your intentions honorable?"

"Certainly. I want to sleep with you. Repeatedly if possible." My intentions went much further than that, actually—but some instinct told me to keep my mouth shut.

"Well, I'm not especially sleepy at the moment—but would you like to fuck?"

"Yes!" Sudden thought. "Uh, I'm fertile."

"I'm covered."

"You're certainly about to be."

When Mickey Finn reprograms reality, he does so with thoughtfulness and subtlety. The heap of clothes we made stayed dry, but now we could feel the warm rain on our bodies—except that nothing could make it run up our noses even when they were upturned. I didn't notice until after; I was preoccupied. She was warm and soft and limber and skilled and *very* enthusiastic; somewhere in there I started believing in God again just to have somebody to thank.

The distant sounds of my friends' voices came drifting up through the roof, and that seemed correct. One of the greatest pleasures in my life is turning people I like on to Callahan's Place; I get a big kick out of introducing a new friend to my old friends. I had never yet turned someone I *loved* on to Callahan's, simply because in the last dozen years I hadn't come to love anyone that I hadn't met in Callahan's, but I expected it to be at least twice as nice— and I already knew that I loved Mary. I was beginning to be *in* love *with* her (if you get the distinction), the first time I'd been in love since I killed my family, and the prospect of introducing a lover to Mike and the gang sounded heavenly. Just a sliver of a thought, this, that resonated every time the faint sound of a familiar laugh reached me, a warm certainty that there could have been no finer place to fall in love, and to make love for the first time, than where I was.

God, she was a sweet pillowy armful! I've had a few of the bony women everyone else claims to like: nothing to squeeze, nothing to admire, I had to be careful with my weight, I was afraid to let go for fear I might bruise something, and even so my pubic bone got sore. A woman like Mary, now: you can *roll around* on a woman like that. You can let yourself go, secure in the awareness that the system is roomy and cushioned, and you can explore forever without running out of things to see and appreciate, and you find, time after time, so often that I'm tempted to say always, that passion and compassion and sensuality each double for every pound above so-called "optimum weight." Take your skinny women and stick them up the same receptacle with hard beds and cold showers and red-line exercise and "natural" food and all the other things everyone earnestly pursues in the belief that pleasure and pain are nature's diabolical attempts to trick us, that the less you enjoy a thing the better it must be for you; take 'em and stick 'em, and give me something a man can enjoy!

Our lovemaking was about as good as a first time can be. It was not the telepathic experience it could become with practice and study, of course—perhaps even less so than a simple sporting event might have been. I spent most of my time in my own head, startled by the unexpected magnitude of my own need, and then bemused by the discovery that hers was even greater. The urgency vs. tenderness ratio definitely tilted to the left, and there seemed to be some question as to who was raping whom. It got pretty athletic in spots. (Doubtless noisy as well, though I'm sure the rain blanketed most of it.) Most of the information that we passed back and forth came directly from the spinal column or just a little bit higher up.

But tenderness was in there too, and caring, and sharing, and something oddly like nostalgia, and so all in all it was about as nice a last time as you could have asked for, too. Our afterglow-durations synched, which is always nice, and we picked little roofing-pebbles from each other's backs, for all the world like monkeys hunting lice. In the process we magically dried out again. It turned out that we both smoked the same brand of cigarette, but when we took two from the pack, Finn's magic selectively failed and they soaked through. We wasted two more before giving up, then I cautiously experimented and learned that a joint was immune. Opinionated man, Finn—but maybe he knows something. We dressed while we toked, and when we were dressed we started drifting over toward the stairwell.

I stopped. "Mary, let's not go down yet. Once we do it'll be wall-to-wall introductions and smiles and drinks and toasts. I want you to meet my friends—but I haven't had a chance to get to know you yet."

"As the old joke goes, it's been the equivalent of a formal introduction."

"You know what I mean. I don't know where you live or where you grew up or what you want to do with your life or how many husbands you have—hell, I don't know your last name!"

"I don't know yours."

"My point exactly. The inmates downstairs, lovable and extraordinary though they be, will keep—let's talk."

"Let's talk later: you know we will. Right now I want to go where there are lights on."

"Yes, but—"

"I want to check the staircase over one more time, too."

"—it's perfectly—"

"All right, I want to hear people admiring it."

"—you don't—"

"I want a drink."

"—I bow to superior intelligence."

Warm light and happy noise and the smell of good suds came flooding out the opened door; as we descended the stairs the sour, oddly pleasant aroma of Callahan's ever-present El Ropo cigars joined the mix. Under the laughter and talk, Fast Eddie Costigan was playing Mac Rebennac stuff, and occasionally one patron or another would scat along with him. Noah Gonzalez was working on a gag he'd picked up from Al Phee, juggling full shot glasses, and by God he finally had it down cold. A small cheering section had gathered; while they clapped, Noah started sipping from the shots as they passed his face. (Noah works for the

Suffolk County Bomb Squad, is why one leg is artificial, and a merrier man you'll never meet.) Mary and I joined the onlookers; true artistry is rare. Noah drained two tumblers, spilling no more than a teaspoon or so on himself, then swallowed, wiped his mouth without losing rhythm, and hollered out, "Open wide, Drink!"

Long-Drink McGonnigle never blows a cue. "Hit me," he cried, and opened his mouth wide.

This is what I think I saw: the shot glass still containing whiskey went up one last time, tilting this time in stately slow motion so that the contents *almost* spilled; then it came down, and Noah caught it, stopped it cold with three fingers, the contents departed on a high trajectory, Noah flung it back into the stream of traffic so that it made up the lost time, we held our collective breath—and the Drink whipped his head two inches to the left and the flying booze impacted squarely against the back of his throat. A roar went up, and Noah laughed so hard he lost all three glasses, and—perhaps most magnificent of all—Long-Drink did *not* lose so much as a drop of the load.

So rarely in life are we privileged to be present at such a moment. When I was ten, my family spent a summer vacation puptenting around New Hampshire, and inevitably we took the cog railway up Mount Washington, a journey itself worth remembering, but what I will never forget as long as I live is standing at the lookoff railing with the family, admiring the view while trying to keep from being blown over the edge by the fierce mountaintop wind, and the truly beautiful thing that happened then. Dad's hat blew off, before he could even try to save it, and sailed out over an indescribable gulf, bound for the state of Maine with every chance of making it. He'd been a little grumpy earlier that day, and had regained his good spirits by force of will only a short time earlier; the rest of us made small cries of dismay as we watched his hat recede. So did several bystanders. But Dad was heroically determined to keep his good mood: he forced a smile, and even essayed a joke. "Don't worry," he called above the wind, "there'll be another one along in a minute." He put up his hand as if to pluck a hat from the sky. And a hat flew into his hand.

This, you may say, and I will agree, is a wonderful thing, a marvelous thing. But the *beautiful* thing, the thing that came back to me again and again during my stormy adolescent battles with Dad and kept me from ever really hating him, is what he did then. He caught the hat, smoothly, and without the slightest hesitation placed it on his head, poker-faced. Even the fact that it was a perfect fit did not faze him. "You see?" he said, and held a deadpan all the way through the ensuing ovation. I've always loved and admired my dad, but in that two or three seconds he became immortal.

Some moments are golden, is what I'm saying, and what Noah had just pulled off was one of those, somebody playing above himself. It made me feel awed and happy and grateful. Callahan's Place had done me proud, serving up some magic for me just as I brought Mary in the door to meet it. After the inevitable storm of glasses had shattered in the fireplace, I joined the throng of people who wanted to buy Noah and Long-Drink a drink. We were all disappointed, as Callahan had caught the act and announced that the boys' tab was covered for the night—but I was mildly annoyed to notice that Mary too had offered the pair a drink . . . from a flask. She had insisted on coming down here, putting off our getting to know each other (*other* than in the biblical sense, I mean), because she wanted a drink—which she'd had with her. We could have sat up there on the roof and killed the flask, talked for hours before coming downstairs . . .

Hush, I told myself sensibly. Sexual intercourse vests no property rights. And how could I resent any combination of circumstances which had allowed me to witness the triumph of Noah and the McGonnigle? All around the room, people whose attention had been elsewhere were getting the tale secondhand and kicking themselves. Let it go, Jake—

"That was special," Mary told me, grinning and taking my hand.

"Yes, indeed. Noah claims he's working up a routine

with live chainsaws, and now I think I believe him. What'll you have?"

She sniffed the air. "Do I smell coffee?"

"Jamaican Blue Mountain. Mike has friends in Tokyo. And, anticipating your next question, he also has Old Bushmill's, distilled in Ireland, and fresh whipped cream, and he knows how. Come on."

Callahan was working up a sweat behind the bar when we got there, but he stopped short as he came past us with twelve drafts in his big hands and said to Mary, gesturing in my direction, "Mary, if your tastes are as simple as this, you might be interested in dating *me* sometime."

"What can I do?" she said. "He's got the negatives. But thanks."

Callahan wrinkled his big broken nose and grimaced. "Damn. Jake, what'll you charge me for a print?"

"Sorry. The rights are tied up. Mike, you sure picked a good staircase-putter-inner. You *do* know where that thing came from?"

"Sure do," Callahan said. "I made a point of asking Sally for it when I heard she was closing. Yeah, Mary does good work. What'll you folks have?"

"God's Blessing on us both, Mike," I told him. He nodded and went off with his dozen overdue beers.

Mary was smiling broadly. "I *like* this place, Jake."

"I already knew you had good taste. Pun intended."

"Ouch. You did warn me."

"Around here we don't even wait for straightlines."

"Well," she said, absolutely pokerfaced, "the shortest distance between two puns is a straightline," and helped herself to some peanuts from the free lunch.

I felt like I had the time I was coming on just a little to a stranger about what a hot guitarist I was, and discovered too late that I was talking to Mr. Amos Garrett. (Remember the demonic guitar break in Maria Muldaur's "Midnight At the Oasis"? *That* Amos Garrett . . .) "And the success of any pun," I tried to riposte, "is in—"

"—the *oy* of the beholder," she finished for me.

Hmmm...

Mike returned with a pair of Irish coffees. "Two God's Blessings," he announced. "I could swear I still hear rain—but you two are bone-dry, and I don't see a brolly."

"Finn's doing," I explained, and he nodded. "Say, Mike, where do you know Mary from? And how come you never invited her around before?"

"Long story. Excuse me, will you? It's time to get the evening started."

He emptied a glass that Shorty Steinitz had foolishly left unattended and banged it on the bartop. "All right, folks—Tall Tales Night is now in session. Who's first?"

Ralph Von Wau Wau was pushed forward by the crowd. "I do have a mildly interesting story for you all," he said, and I glanced at Mary to see how she would take it. I mean, I suppose it's a subjective thing, but I find a talking dog to be more intrinsically startling than a seven-foot flying cyborg. But she didn't blink. Well, I had warned her.

In that charming German accent of his (he *is* a Shepherd), Ralph told a fairly complex story about a demonically possessed lady of his acquaintance whom he had exorcised after even a bishop had failed; the yarn built inexorably, to the line, "Possession is nine points of the paw," and produced some very canine howls of agony from the innocent bystanders.

Which of course only inspired Doc Webster. "Damned if I'll be outpunned by a genuine son of a bitch," he boomed, and folks made way grinning for him as he stepped forward. Physically the Doc resembles a Sumo wrestler gone to fat. He is the All-time Punday Night Champion and probably always will be; only Long-Drink and I still cherish a hope of supplanting him anymore.

"As many of you know," the Doc began, "I just got back from visiting Juan Ortiz, an obstetrician friend of mine in Los Angeles. He was nominally on vacation, but one day there was an emergency delivery he just had to attend, so he deputized his brother-in-law Obie Stihl—honest to God, that's his name, I'd never make up a name like that—

deputized Obie to show me around town. We went to Disneyland. Obie turned out to be a dedicated Star Wars freak, with a sense of humor even more depraved than my own—we passed by three sailors on the way in, for instance, and when he noticed they were all Chief Petty Officers, he made sure to point out the 'Three C.P.O.s'..." (sounds of gagging and dismay from the audience). "So he took me to Adventureland, where you go on a Jungle Boat Ride. Robot hippos come up out of the water and spit at you and so forth." ("Maybe they were relatives of yours," Long-Drink murmured, and Callahan shushed him.) "But the worst part was the damned boat captain. Through the whole voyage he kept up a running monologue that had shin splints: bad jokes, worse puns, mother-in-law jokes even. I was in severe pain; fella thought he was a real hot dog. But the wurst was yet to come." (Gasps.) "As we got back to the wharf, just as I was stepping off the boat, Obie leaned over and whispered in my ear, 'Now you're getting to see the dock side of the farce...'"

A roar of collective anguish went up, and glasses began to fly toward the hearth. "Rest of us might as well fold up," Tommy Janssen said. "That's a winner."

"Strictly speaking," Callahan said with some reluctance, "I'm afraid it ain't. That story'd probably take the honors if this was Punday Night—but I don't really see it as a Tall Tale."

"He's right," Long-Drink said. "It's nice if the Tall Tale ends with a crime like that, but the Tale itself has to have fantastic elements to it. Sorry, Doc: syntax error."

The Doc frowned, but what could he say? They were right. And then divine fire touched me, as it had Noah a while earlier.

I wanted to impress my new love, and I wanted to help Doc Webster, and it just slipped out before I knew I was going to speak: "I'm surprised at you boys. The fantastic element in that story is staring you all right in the face."

Even the Doc looked puzzled. "How's that, Jake?" Callahan asked.

"Well, how many of you have ever toured Disneyland, or anyplace else, with a fictional character?"

The Doc was the only one who saw it coming; his frown left.

"Doc *told* you who his guide was: O.B. Juan's kin, Obie."

A frozen silence. Group catatonic shock. And then Ralph began to howl, and was joined by the rest. Every glass in the room, full or empty, began a journey whose terminus was the fireplace; Eddie tried to play the Star Wars theme but was laughing so hard he couldn't get his hands to agree on a key; Callahan reached threateningly for a seltzer bottle; Doc Webster shook my hand respectfully.

I glanced around for Mary to see if she was suitably impressed, and found her staring across the room. I followed her gaze, realized she was staring at Finn—and realized that Finn was in some kind of trouble.

He was sitting bolt upright in his chair, which he hardly ever does, being so tall, and he was paying no attention to the proceedings around him, and tears were running down his face. The last time I'd seen tears on Finn's face, years before, the planet Earth had been in serious jeopardy...

He got up and walked stiffly to the bar, and Mary and I moved wordlessly to where we could see what Finn was doing.

He was offering Mike Callahan ten singles. He wanted ten of something. Callahan was looking him over. "How much effect will that have on him?" Mary asked in a whisper.

"About like you or I gulping a double."

"Oh." She relaxed slightly.

"But it is *extremely* out of character for Finn. The last time I saw him order ten drinks was the first night he came here, years ago."

"*Oh.*"

Many others at or near the bar knew the story; an audience was developing as Callahan reached his decision. "What'll it be, Mickey?"

"Rye, Michael." Just like that night.

"You want to talk about it?" Callahan asked.

"First the toast."

Callahan nodded at that, and set to work. He builds drinks the way Baryshnikov dances. Ten shots of rye soon sat before Finn. One after another the tall alien downed them. That first night he had thrown each individual empty into the fireplace and made the same toast ten times; this time he didn't bother. When he was done, some of the empties weren't even touching—but he picked the last one up and the rest came with it. He walked to the chalk line, faced the hearth. By now he had our attention.

"To my people," he said clearly and tonelessly, and flung the cluster of glasses.

I hadn't known even Finn could throw that hard: there was a violent explosion in the fireplace. It is designed like a parabolic reflector, so that it is nearly impossible to make glass spray out of it; nonetheless, that bursting should have littered the room with shards. It did not for the same reason that my clothes were dry.

"Jesus, big fella," Long-Drink said. "What can we do?" There was a vigorous rumble of agreement on all sides.

Mickey Finn came back to Earth—an expression perhaps uniquely appropriate here—and looked around at us gravely. His composed features were at odds with the droplets running down them; I had the crazy thought that these were the raindrops that had failed to fall on him, time-shifted somehow to now. But of course it was just that Finn's still not used to hanging human expressions on his pan, and tends to forget in times of crisis: he truly was hurting.

"My friends," he told us, "if I could think of anything you could do, I would surely tell you. Would surely have told you before now."

"Then tell us the problem," Tommy Janssen said. "Maybe we'll come up with something."

Finn tried a smile, a poor job. "I doubt it, Tommy. I have been thinking about this particular problem since I first came here, years ago, and I do not think there is a solution."

Callahan cleared his throat, a sound like a speeding truck being thrown suddenly into reverse. "Mickey, as you know, I don't hold with pryin' in my joint. If you don't feel like telling us your troubles, I'll coldcock the first guy that asks a leading question. But I strongly recommend that you unload. Little thing you might not know, having spent so many centuries alone out in deep space: sometimes, just naming your burden helps. But it's up to you, pal."

Finn thought it over. "You may be right, Michael. You always have been so far. In fact, you have stated my problem. *I am alone*. I have been alone for centuries. I shall always be alone, until my death comes."

"The hell you say," Long-Drink burst out. "Why, counting the regulars that ain't in tonight, I make it about a hundred and fifty close friends you've got. You can stay at my crib anytime, for as long as you like, and the same goes for the rest of us, ain't that right?"

There were universal shouts of agreement. Finn smiled a pained smile. "Thank you all," he said. "You are true friends. But your generous offer does not speak to my problem. I did not say I was lonely. I said I was *alone*."

"Mickey," Josie Bauer began silkily, "I told you once already—"

"Again, thanks," he said, sketching a gallant bow. "But it would, forgive me, hurt more than it would help."

"Hurt how?" she asked, not in the least offended.

"Physically, for one thing, it would hurt *you*. You recall the Niven story you lent me once, about Superman's sex life?"

"'Man of Steel, Woman of Kleenex', sure," she said. *"Oh."*

"Yes," Finn said sadly. "Orgasm involves involuntary muscle spasm—and while I am not as strong as Superman, I am much stronger than a Terran man. And you are slightly built."

"Oh."

There was something peculiar about Finn's face. The

eyes, that was it. His eyes hadn't looked like that since the first night he'd come here. Hollow, burnt out, empty of all hope. Why hadn't they looked like that up on the roof? Or had I just failed to notice in the dark, distracted by lust? "It would hurt me, too," he went on. "Not physically—spiritually. Human females often become angry when I try to explain this, Josie, *please* do not be offended, but would it not be fair to say that what you were just about to offer me was a transient sexual relationship?"

"Now, hold on a goddam—"

"I *said*, 'Please', Josie."

"—uh . . . dammit, Finn, I didn't mean a purely sexual—"

"Of course not; I do not believe myself that there is any such thing. No doubt it would have involved friendship and laughter and kindness and several other wonderful qualities for which you Terrans do not yet have words. But is not the key word 'transient'?"

"Well, for crying out—"

"I am wrong? You were proposing marriage?"

Josie shut very quickly up.

"Perhaps your subconscious intent was a liaison of days, or weeks, or even months. But I am sure that you were not offering to become my *mate*. No human ever would."

"Christ, Mickey, don't run yourself down. I don't happen to be the marrying kind, but I'm sure that some nice g—"

"Look at me," he roared suddenly, and everyone in the Place jumped a foot in the air. Deliberately, he pulled open his black sports coat, pulled open his shirt, pulled open his chest . . .

I tried to look away, could not. I tried to fit words around what I was seeing, could not. I tried not to be horrified, could not. A strange sound filled the room: many people sucking air through their teeth. I can't describe it, even now: take my word for it, whatever was inside Finn's chest, human beings aren't supposed to see things like that. Ever.

Finn closed up his chest.

A collective sigh went up.

"I have shown you my heart," Finn said softly. "Will you marry me?"

Josie began to whimper.

"Josie, I am sorry," he said at once, but it was too late—she was out the door and gone. He said a word then which I've never heard before and hope never to hear again, something in his native tongue that hurt him worse than it did us. Josie's a real nice lady, and Finn knew it.

Callahan cleared his throat.

"Mickey," he rumbled, "you're alone, we get it now. It's a hard thing to be alone. Everyone in here has been alone, some of us are now—"

"Not as I am," Finn stated. "Even the most unfortunate of you is less alone. Now matter how remote the chance of your finding a mate...there is always the *chance*. Always you have hope, even as you despair. No human will ever pair-bond with me—and I dare not leave your planet. My Masters believe me dead; if they ever learned otherwise—"

"—they'd kill you," Long-Drink finished.

"Worse."

"They'd punish you."

"Worse."

"What's worse?" Shorty Steinitz asked.

"They would put me back to work, unpunished. They are not like humans, who sometimes kick a machine that is not working. They would simply restore the machine to service. And, as an afterthought, they would exterminate the organisms which caused the machine to malfunction."

"Us, you mean," Callahan said.

"Yes."

Mary and Callahan exchanged a look I didn't understand. "There's no chance you could sneak back to your home planet without these Master clowns catching on?" she asked Finn.

"None whatsoever," Finn said expressionlessly. "To begin with, my home planet no longer exists. It has not existed for several centuries, and I am the last of my people."

Mary winced. "What happened?"

"The Masters found us."

"Jesus—and killed everybody but you."

"They killed everybody *including* me. But the Masters are a prudent and tidy race; they always keep file copies of what they destroy, each etched on a molecule of its own. Like all of my people, I was slain, and reduced to a single encoded molecule. Some time after my death they felt need of a new scout, fashioned this body, and caused to be decanted into it a large fraction of my former awareness— withholding the parts that did not suit them, of course."

Mary gasped; she was horrified. "God, you must hate them."

Finn's voice was bleak. "I wish greatly that I had the ability. That is one of the parts that did not suit them."

I was as horrified as Mary. As a rule, Finn is disinclined to talk about his past, and of course none of us had ever tried to pry. I'd always wondered how he'd gotten into his former profession. Now I was sorry I knew.

(Still, I was tempted to ask him the other thing that had always puzzled me: why the body he wore looked human. Was human stock ubiquitous through the Galaxy? Had his Masters designed him specifically to come *here?* Or did he somehow reform his body for each new planet, each new culture? I knew that at least half his body was organic— but did that half have anything in common with the body he had been born into?

Perhaps the answer was equally horrifying. In any case, my friend Finn was in pain: This was no time to be snoopy.)

"Mickey," Mary said softly, "if you are unable to hate your Masters . . . then you are unable to love them. Yes? That's why you were able to betray them."

"Yes. They do not wish to be loved. They would find the idea disgusting. Love baffles and repels them, they stamp it out wherever they find it in the Galaxy. The Masters are motivated by self-interest."

"So are most humans," Mary said.

Finn actually laughed. "Excuse me, Mary my new friend, but what you said is funny. *All humans—without exception—want to love*. No organic or emotional or psychological damage can remove that need. Humans can survive, albeit in pain, without *being* loved—but lock a man in a dungeon and he will find an ant to love, or try. The sociopath, who feels no emotions, wishes he could, and is driven mad by his inability. Love is the condition in which the happiness and welfare of another are essential to your own. To any rational selfish mind, this is insanity. To a Master it would be obscenity: perhaps the corresponding horror for a human being would be ego-death."

"Love *is* ego-death," Mary whispered.

"The Masters have run across love from time to time in their expansion through the Galaxy. They're not at all afraid that it might infect *them,* nor do I believe that to be a possibility, but they always exterminate it with a special pleasure, a *frisson* of horror, a small thrill of disgust." Finn closed his eyes briefly. "It was the flaw for which my race died."

The Place was silent. Mary's fingers were digging painfully into my arm, and I couldn't protest because I was gripping her arm just as hard. Why was she glaring at Callahan?

"When first we encountered the Masters, we considered the problem they represented and evolved two possible solutions. One involved their complete annihilation, root, stock, and branch; the other was more risky. We loved Life, and especially Sentience, and they were sentient. We took the risk and were destroyed. Perhaps it was the wrong choice.

"In any case, I am nearly all that remains of my race, and so I am disinclined to die. I can neither love nor hate my Masters, but I can fear them and do."

"It must have been hard for you to quit them," Mary said.

"Yes, but not because of the fear. That came later. It was hard because I am only partly organic. I contain installations, which were programmed by the Masters. Betrayal was almost a physical impossibility for me: I was *counter-programmed*. With an effort that burned out small components and may have taken a century off my lifespan, I was barely able to *hint* at how my programming might be circumvented—and these my friends were able to interpret my hints and act on them."

"Aren't your . . . Mick, I'm sorry, I just can't use that word. Aren't the Cockroaches likely to notice you're gone and come looking for you?"

"No, Mary. The Galaxy is a big dark place, and the . . . Cockroaches, being rational, are cautious. If a scout fails to report in, the area he was exploring is left alone. My defensive systems are mighty; it would take a powerful enemy to destroy me without my consent."

Callahan set up another five shots. "Finn," he asked, "tell me if it's none o' my business, but is it possible for you to suicide?"

"No, Michael. Or I would have done so, before I ever came to your tavern that first night." He downed two of the shots. "But, as with my loyalty to the Cockroaches . . . thank you for that name, Mary . . . my will to live can be tampered with slightly. I could not suicide—but given the right conditions and a strong enough motivation, I could cooperate in my assassination." He finished the remaining shots. "You will recall that on that first night here, I begged you all to kill me."

"No, Mickey," Callahan said softly. "I don't recall that." He trod his cigar underfoot and lit a new one. "I don't ever plan to, either. One more personal question?"

"Of course, Michael."

It was a ten-cent cigar or worse, but Mike took his time getting it lit properly. "You said, 'strong enough motivation.'" Puff. "Tell me, buddy . . ." Puff. ". . . is loneliness a strong enough motivation?"

Not a chair creaked; not a sleeve rustled; not a glass clinked. The fire seemed to quiet in the hearth; the rain seemed to have stopped. Somewhere in there Mary and I had lost our grip on each other's arm; I wanted to get mine back, but something told me to stay still.

Finn sighed finally, and put ten more singles on the bar-top. Callahan handed him a fresh fifth, and while he was drinking off the top quarter of it, Callahan said quickly and quietly, "Mickey, once upon a time you had a problem you couldn't solve, and dying looked like the only way out. But you kept on looking for another way out, and in the pro-verbial nick of time you found one."

Finn wiped his mouth with his long forearm. "Michael, I have been looking for a solution to this problem for a long time. All the time I have been on Earth. I think very quickly. In the same amount of time I could have deduced this solar system from one of your cigar stubs."

"Mickey," Mary began, and then caught herself. "Mickey Finn isn't your real name, is it?"

"Yes, it is, but in the sense you mean you are correct: it is not the birthname my father gave me."

"What is your birthname?"

Finn smiled sadly. "You couldn't pronounce it."

"Try me."

He started to argue but gave in and spoke his name. When I'd heard it I agreed with him. The closest I can render it is "Txffu Mpwfs." Whatever Finn's people had been like, I was sure their mouths were constructed differ-ently than ours.

Mary got it dead-bang perfect the first time. "Txffu," she said, "weren't you just as lonely, or lonelier, when you worked for the Roaches? It must be a long time between star systems."

Finn blinked at hearing his name on another's lips for the first time in—how long? —but was distracted by her question. "For one thing, there was always the tiny but measurable possibility that the . . . the Roaches might have reactivated others of my race to become scouts, that I might, if I lived long enough, chance to meet such a one eventually, that we might—" He broke off and did more damage to his fifth. "There was hope. Microscopic hope, perhaps, but hope. But now I must stay here, and no other of my race will ever come, and there is no hope."

He looked at the bottle. It was almost empty. Perhaps he sympathized with it; he put it down unfinished. "And when I worked for the Mas—for the Cockroaches, I had a job. A function. A purpose. A less than totally desirable one, admittedly. But I was part of something greater than myself, and I had a role to play. What is my role here on Earth? I have tried to anchor myself to this planet, to 'put down roots'—I have pursued farming and fishing and hunting and several other most basic trades. I can imitate a terrestrial organism in general and a human in particular.

"But I am alien. I have no purpose here, no job which needs me to do it. This makes my loneliness all the sharper. Perhaps I could stand loneliness if I were not useless; perhaps I could stand uselessness if I were not lonely." His voice was eerily calm and flat as he finished, "The two together are more than I can bear."

The silence that ensued then was a familiar one. Someone names a problem—an act similar in many ways to giving birth—and then the rest of us sit around a while in respectful, sympathetic, contemplative silence, admiring the newborn little monster and meditating ways to kill it. Although it's difficult to read a man who has facial and vocal expressions and body language only when he remembers to, I felt that Finn had completed his birthing, and I put my mind on solutions for his problems. This was going to be one of the longer silences.

I've tried my hand at matchmaking a few times, and learned that you should approach it like walking into a chemistry lab and mixing two unidentified beakers of chemicals: you might luck into a stable compound, or you might blow your hands off. I'm willing to take the risk for a good enough friend, and Finn qualified—but where do you find a mate for someone as uniquely alien as him? And in today's job market, how much demand was there for a fellow whose principal prior job experience involved locating and sterilizing planetary systems? I came up with a few dozen trial solutions, rejected them all, realized how little chance I had of finding one that Finn had not considered and rejected months or years ago.

But I was being premature. "Txffu," Mary said, "that isn't all of it, is it?"

He spun his head to look at her. Those eyes of his seemed to smolder.

"Mary," Callahan said reproachfully, "That's all he chose to tell us. We don't pry in here, you know that."

"He's asking us to fix two legs of a three-legged stool, Mike. I don't do work like that."

"Then sit this one out. But no pryin' questions in my joint. It's up to him whether to show you his legs or not."

She turned back to Finn. "As a card-carrying Sophist, I will now proceed to make some prying *statements*, and if you choose to react to any of them it won't be my place to stop you.

"The third leg of your stool, you stool, is called fear. I don't mean your fear of the Cockroaches, you've learned to live with that. Something else has you scared, and for some reason you don't want to talk about it. Not because you're afraid to admit you're afraid, like human males; it's something else. I for one would certainly like to hear about it."

Finn tilted his head slightly to one side. "I see further into the infrared than humans, hear an extra octave on either side of human range. Do you see emotions others cannot perceive?"

She ignored the question. "You're stalling."

He closed his eyes briefly—I welcomed the momentary respite—and made his decision.

"Very well. I am afraid of the same thing that everyone in this room is afraid of."

Long-Drink McGonnigle nodded. "Death."

"No, Drink my friend. I do not fear death. Neither do some others in this room. I fear Apocalypse. Armageddon. Ragnarok and Fimbulwinter. I fear nuclear holocaust."

There was a murmur in Callahan's Place.

• • •

"Finn," Doc Webster said, "do you have reason to believe that it's coming?"

"No more reason than anyone else here, Sam," Finn assured him. "Is that not sufficient?"

"What's it to *you*, Mickey?" Mary asked suddenly.

"Mary!" I said, scandalized—no, shocked and dismayed.

It was her tone of voice, you see, the way she was coming on strong with Finn. If Callahan had said those words, in that tone, it would have been different. Lots of times I've seen him appear to bully someone into solving their own problem, adopt a gruff, belligerent manner as a way of getting through their self-involvement. The rest of us are a mite too sympathetic sometimes. But when he does it, we all know that it's just Callahan, that he's simply using rudeness, as a way—an effective way—of loving.

But Mary was a stranger here. In a sense she had not yet earned the right to talk that way in here, to a friend of ours. Perhaps if she herself had already opened up to us in some way, aired some problem and been adopted by us, it would have been different. (But that sounded silly even as I was thinking it: what, did people have to show a scab at the door to get admitted to Callahan's Place?) All I knew was that it wasn't right for her to be using that harsh, challenging, almost cruel tone of voice with my friend Finn. And that dismayed me, because it was my first suggestion that maybe I did not know Mary as well as I thought I did.

"I just want to get it straight," Mary insisted. "Mick, Jake told me earlier you've studied a few stars—*from inside*. If you can survive in the heart of a fusion furnace, what do you care about a little thing like Armageddon?"

"It would destroy you and all your kind!" Finn said.

"So? You told us just a few minutes ago that the Cockroaches left you unable to hate or love."

"They left me unable to hate or love *them!*" he said forcefully. "I can love. I can love humankind. I do."

"Uh-huh," she said nastily, and Finn's face twisted and my heart turned over within me.

"Mary," I said quickly, "You don't know what you're talking about—"

"Shut up, please, Jake," she said. "Mick, why—"

"No, you shut up," I snapped. "He betrayed his Masters for us, he exiled himself here to save us, he *proved* his love—and again when the Krundai came, he fought for us! You don't know, you weren't here, you have no right, you don't know him—"

"Mick is your friend, and you told me about him for fifteen minutes—if you forgot to tell me the important parts it's not my fault. Now I asked you to shut up, and I said 'please'. Look here, Finn, you noble spaceman—"

I shut up and let her browbeat my friend. I was busy trying to fall out of love.

(A rotten little voice in the back of my head was asking, are you sure you want to lose a body like that just to keep your self-respect? and I had to admit it was a good, if swinish, question.)

"—if you claim you quit your job out of love for humanity, and you claim to be scared of Apocalypse on our account, then why the hell is it that you haven't done one goddam thing to prevent it?"

Finn opened his mouth.

"And if you give me the Star Trek Prime Directive," she cut him off, "I'll spit right in your eye. Nobody who really cared about the ethics of interfering in the destinies of primitive cultures could ever have worked as an interstellar hit man—conditioning and counterprogramming be damned!"

"It is not that I would not prevent nuclear catastrophe," Finn said. "I cannot."

"Bullshit."

"I can destroy nuclear weapons easily. But I cannot destroy *every*one, simultaneously, and anything less would only trigger the calamity."

"Oh, for Christ's sake, Mick—you're not that dumb. You could think your way around the problem in about thirty seconds flat ... if you weren't hamstrung by guilt."

"Guilt?"

"That's right. Resolve the conflict in your conscience,

and everything else will fall into place, you wait and see."

"—'conflict?'—"

"For years, now, ever since you first walked into this dump, you've been taking credit for saving the world out of love of humanity—and these chumps here bought it." She glared around at all of us, ignored the glares she got in return, and turned back to Finn. *"Why don't you tell us the real reason?"*

And she got him! I was watching his face, and Finn may not have much human expression, but I know a direct hit when I see one. She knew something, she'd seen something we hadn't. I tried to do an emotional one-eighty, and got so disoriented I nearly missed Finn's reply.

At first it didn't look like there was going to be one. He froze up like a computer that's lost its cursor. People speak of someone "turning to stone"—but I don't think any human being could have come as close as Finn to doing that literally. Three or four seconds went by like zeppelins in a desultory breeze . . . and then suddenly he was shouting:

"All right, damn it: I am not immortal!"

The volume made the windows ring and people wince. Motorists may well have heard him out on 25A, rain and all. As the echo of his shout died away, Mary said, quite softly, "I figured it was something like that. You're going to be needing maintenance pretty soon, aren't you?"

Finn sighed and spoke in his normal voice. "If I do not receive fairly extensive maintenance within approximately two hundred and twenty years, I will experience critical systems failures. I will die. It is a trick of the Masters, another way to prevent their scouts deserting as I've done. When I arrived on this planet, I estimated that humanity could possess the necessary technological sophistication within a century or two . . . if it survived that long. If you had been less advanced, you would have been no use to me; more advanced, and you would have detected my approach and perhaps fired upon me. The 'window' was open. Your political immaturity made you a most dangerous gamble—but you were the best chance I had seen in countless millennia. I staked everything on you."

Callahan poured himself a shot of Bushmill's and tossed it back. "What kind of maintenance, Mickey? Organic or cybernetic?"

"Both, Michael. And one other kind for which your people do not yet have a name."

"Why'n'cha just teach it to us?"

Finn shook his head. "Could you have taught Leonardo Da Vinci to build a railroad before it was railroading time?"

"So that first night you came in here, all of that was a charade?"

"No, Michael! Not at all. I meant it when I asked you to . . . well, you say you don't remember that. In any case, you refused to do it then. I was in agony. I realized that I had a chance to survive on this world—but I was programmed to transmit my observations of humanity to the Masters at a preset time, and I knew that when I had I would receive orders to sterilize your planet. I could not countermand that programming. The irony was crushing. It was only when you asked me my name that the idea came to me: if I could give you enough hint, you could drug me unconscious and prevent my transmission for me. And I managed to do so, and you took the hint."

"But I mean, you didn't defect and save us for the reason you said, because you learned here that humans have love? You did it because we might get smart enough one day to keep your motor tuned for you? Is that the size of it?"

Finn didn't hang his head; his people must not have had that custom. "My decision was predicated solely on self-interest, Michael. I *was* pleased to find that you had love—because it would make it easier to get you to help me, when one day you could."

Shorty Steinitz was wearing the same look he'd had the day he broke Weasel Wetzel's face-bone—and Shorty *knows* that Finn could outpunch an F-111. "Let me get this straight, Finn," he said darkly. "You don't love the human race?"

"Oh hell, Shorty," Long-Drink said, *"I* don't love the human race, comes to that. There's an ever-dwindlin' percentage I can *tolerate.*"

"All right," Shorty insisted, "this *place*, then, these peo-

ple . . . Finn, are you sayin' you got no love for Callahan's
Place here? For us?"

Finn started to answer, and paused as Tommy Janssen
shouldered his way forward. The kid's voice was low and
soft and dangerous. "You came in here the night these guys
got me off smack," he said, "and you watched them save
me, watched while they sewed my balls back on, and then
you got up and did your little dance *because you figured it
was cheap medical insurance?* I'm the youngest guy here,
twenty-five, if I quit smoking I might live another fifty,
sixty years—*if* the goddam bomb doesn't go off tomorrow.
Some of the other people here . . . hell, Tom Flannery's *died*
since the night you came in here. And you're worried about
Apocalypse because it might cut you back to another two
or three centuries of sunrises? Now, where did I put my
violin?"

God help me, I spoke up. "Finn—all these years we've
been knockin' our brains out trying to make you feel at
home in a strange land, helping you get papers and teaching
you about baseball and trying to teach you how to sing and
all that . . . all that time you were just *using* us?"

I shut up then, because Finn's feelings had become so
violent as to reach the surface of his face. One thing apparently all humanoid life forms have in common: the grimace of extreme anguish.

"This is not fair," he roared, and flung his bottle of rye
into the fireplace.

SMASH! Cracks appeared in some of the bricks.

There was a general murmur rising in the room now, but
Mary's soft laughter cut right through it, deflating it. I
turned, to look at her with new eyes. I resented her for
being privy to this intimate matter, for having provoked this
hassle, for being cruel to my friend the rotten son of a bitch
. . . Pushy, and nasty, and castrating, and *fat* . . .

I transferred to her all my conflict; as I had on the roof,
I poured my need into her.

And this time she didn't accept it. I opened my mouth
to say something or other that would end our affair, and

she ignored me, spoke directly and only to Finn.

"Now you're getting it," she said, smiling. "It *isn't* fair. Enjoying it, Mick? Have I given you enough, now? Have you got a way to store it digitally and play it back later? Can you put it on a loop and run it continuously or something?"

He blinked at her.

"You marinate in guilt soup for enough years, you suck all the juice right out of it, have to go get some new vegetables to throw into the pot, that's understandable. But eventually you'll use up this bag. What'll we do next—spread the news around, put you on the Phil Donahue Show? Sooner or later, somebody'd figure out a way to kill you, and you know it, too, you big dumb jerk. Can't you make this last you for a while?"

These were hammer blows she was landing, from a distance of about a foot and a half. I opened my mouth to say something, and suddenly she whirled around to face us. Finn's got a more efficient speaker than any human, but she certainly had an impressive bellow onto her—we jumped further than we had when he let go.

"Will you clowns stop indulging him now?"

The dust settled, Callahan picked his cigar butt up off the floor and blew sawdust off it, and she cut back to about Force Eight and went on:

"What is the *matter* with you morons? A mutt comes in here, a guy you claim is your friend, with a sign on his forehead says, 'Masochist', and you people get out the whips and chains, is that it? Txffu's committed the cardinal sin, eh? He doesn't love humanity: hang him. And Handsome over there, too, and half the people in this bar, probably . . . what the hell is so special about humanity that not loving it is a sin? Finn said his people loved sentient life: I respect that a lot more, and I'm not at all sure that humanity qualifies, on average—"

(By "Handsome," she referred to Long-Drink, whose name she didn't know, and I found time to wonder if Mary was a pervert, too, queer for scrawny men. Long-Drink is even taller and skinnier than me—put him and me and Finn side by side and we look like a pine mountainside . . .)

"—How about an analogy: will that strain your brains too much? Say you work for a South American real estate developer; he has you go out into the bush and exterminate tribes of monkeys where he wants to build new condominiums. You don't like the work, you'd rather quit and jungle up, but the boss has thoughtfully planted a booby-trapped transceiver on you. To make matters worse, you're a diabetic, and he only gives you a limited supply of insulin for each trip.

"One day you run across a tribe of monkeys clever enough to disable the transceiver. It may even be possible to train them to manufacture insulin. *Is it necessary that you love them before you can accept their aid?* I could maybe, given time, learn to get attached to three or four individual monkeys, maybe as many as a dozen or so—be amused by them, grow fond of them, even respect them in certain ways. I could see being concerned if I learned that their tribe was locked into some kind of suicidal behavior pattern—really concerned, not just on my own account. But *love* them? Or their kind in general?

"And should I be ashamed for wanting insulin so that I can live another forty or fifty years—when the monks can only hope for ten or twenty? Oh, you jackasses, I can understand *HIM* being that dumb, he's smarter than any of us— but how could you *morons* be so stupid?"

Many feet were shuffled. She had opened up our friend's hidden wound . . . and we had all picked at it. I was belatedly beginning to realize her technique. Sometimes a mocking voice whispers vile things in a man's ear, things he can't shut out because he half-believes they're true. But if you can *personify* that voice, and get him to fight it, to reject it . . .

"He comes from a race so fatheaded noble and ethical that they couldn't bring themselves to destroy their assassins—*perhaps*, he says, they made the wrong choice. Naturally he'd feel guilty about exploiting us by trying to keep us alive, about his inability to love monkeys. All the years he's been on this planet, none of you noticed any pattern in the kind of professions he's followed?"

I found that I was speaking. "I figured he picked basic, earthy trades as a way of rooting himself to this planet. Our primal cultural basics: farming, fishing, watching the forest, contemplating the sea—"

"Solitary, lonely jobs, every one, the way he went about them. Hermit jobs." She turned to Finn. "You probably find most of us actually repellent, don't you, Txffu?"

His face was expressionless again. "Candidly, yes."

"Physically disgusting?"

"Well . . . deformed, on the average. Your males are all so *short* . . . and your females are all so undernourished . . ."

Her ears grew points. "Really?"

"Yes. Among my people, you yourself would be considered—well, not emaciated, but almost unfashionably slender. As it happens, I have an unconventional taste for slender women . . . but most human females your size hate themselves so much it is unpleasant to be near them—"

"Txffu?" she interrupted.

"Yes, Mary?"

"Will you marry me?"

I screwed my eyes so tight I saw neon paisley. Somewhere behind their lids was the switch that would turn my breathing back on, and I had to find it pretty quickly.

Finn was utterly still for five long seconds. "You are not serious."

"No, thank God, and that's going to be a break for you in the years to come—but my proposal is dead serious. What's your answer?"

"But you—"

"Finn, you've been unable to love because you haven't loved yourself because you haven't loved us—it's time somebody got you off the loop. You ninny, of course you didn't save us out of love! You did it out of *compassion*. That's something that's underrated, but I think it's just as good as love—who knows, maybe better. You can love only your equals—with your superiors or inferiors, compassion is the best you can do, and it's pretty damned good, at least as high up on the ethical scale. With time, it can lead to love. I speculate that it could even be the basis of a pretty fair marriage. Do you think?"

"You saw what is in my chest—"

"Yeah, I'm fascinated. Is there an owner's manual for it?"

"You cannot be serious. You do not even know if we are sexually compatible—"

"The hell I don't. I can see fingers and a tongue from here; anything else is gravy. And I've got *some*thing or other that appeals to you; I knew that back up on the roof when I met you."

That breathing switch had to be around here someplace; just a question of finding it . . .

"—we are not cross-fertile—," Finn tried.

"What of it? Maybe we'll adopt. Hell, we'll adopt this whole goddam bar—they need *someone* to bring 'em up. Quit stalling: yes or no?"

I think maybe I'd known it all along, sensed it up there on the roof when Finn first flew out of the rainy night. I suppose there are worse ways to say goodbye . . .

"Yes," Finn said finally. "Yes, Mary, I would be honored to marry you. On one condition." He turned to the rest of us. "*All* of you, male and female, must agree to be my Best Man."

A roomful of people looked guiltily to Mary.

She nodded serenely. "Deal."

A cheer went up that rung the rafters. I even got my lungs going in time to join it. Sure it hurt.

But it felt good, too.

Finn's face remained blank for another few seconds—and then he remembered to share his joy with us, and hung that expression on himself; I was pleased and proud that he took the trouble.

"Would you two," Callahan boomed, "do me the honor

of gettin' married here in my joint? Say, over there on the staircase?"

"Where else?" Mick and Mary said together, and another cheer went up, even louder.

It came to me that I might find some use for a bucket of alcohol, so when Callahan began the bucket brigade of free drinks for the house I hogged three or four. It's amazing how fast you can throw down booze if you work at it, and so before long I found myself bellying up to the bar.

"Innkeeper," I said when he reached me, "give me drink."

He understood my situation—had probably understood from the moment Mary popped the question. Not much gets past Mike Callahan, and nothing that pertains to the human heart. "Healthy reaction," he said, nodding judiciously. "I think you'll live, Jake."

"Have you ever hated your best friend's guts, Mike?"

"Careful, pal: don't get into the same guilt-loop Finn did. Melodrama is for T.V. Finn's not your best friend, just a garden variety pal. And if you feel like hating him for a while, go to it: it'll pass."

"You haven't said much tonight, Mike. How do *you* feel about all this?"

"Well, the way I look at it, I'm not so much losing a daughter as I am gaining an alien."

I stared at him, and by the time all the tumblers had finished clicking into place, he was handing me an oversized mug of Irish coffee.

"Mary is your—"

"Lady Sally and I have always been real proud of her," he said contentedly, puffing on that miserable stogie.

"Why the hell didn't she ever come around here before?" I asked. "All these years—"

"Well, she couldn't, Jake. She lived too far away, and she used to work nights. Until Sal retired..."

You burn your tongue when you drink Irish coffee too fast, so I burned my tongue. So I had another to keep my tongue numb, and then another, and I started having so much fun that the idea sort of caught on generally, and that's more or less how Mike and I and about a dozen of our friends eventually ended up naked in the rain on Callahan's roof, me for the second time that night.

Do you know, from that day to this, rain won't land on me—or any of us that were there—unless we ask it to?

CHAPTER 2

Pyotr's Story

TWO TOTAL DRUNKS in a single week is much higher than average for anyone who goes to Callahan's Place—no pun intended.

Surely there is nothing odd about a man going to a bar in search of oblivion. Understatement of the decade. But Callahan's Place is what cured me of being a lush, and it's done the same for others. Hell, it's helped keep Tommy Janssen off of *heroin* for years now. I've gotten high there, and once or twice I've gotten tight, but it's been a good many years since I've been flat-out, helpless drunk—or yearned to be. A true drunk is a rare sight at Callahan's. Mike Callahan doesn't just pour his liquor, he serves it; to get pissed in his Place you must convince him you have a need to, persuade him to take responsibility for you. Most bars, people go to in order to get blind. Mike's customers go there to see better.

But that night I had a need to completely dismantle my higher faculties, and he knew that as I crossed the threshold. Because I was carrying in my arms the ruined body of Lady Macbeth. Her head dangled crazily, her proud neck broken clean through, and a hush fell upon Callahan's Place as the door closed behind me.

Mike recovered quickly; he always does. He nodded, a nod which meant both hello and something else, and glanced up and down the bar until he found an untenanted stretch. He pointed to it, I nodded back, and by the time I reached it he had the free lunch and the beer nuts moved out of the way. Not a word was said in the bar—everyone there under-

stood my feelings as well as Callahan did. Do you begin
to see how one could stop being an alcoholic there? Someone, I think it was Fast Eddie, made a subvocal sound of
empathy as I laid the Lady on the bar-top.

I don't know just how old she is. I could find out by
writing the Gibson people and asking when serial number
427248 was sent out into the world, but somehow I don't
want to. Somewhere in the twenty-to-thirty range, I'd guess,
and she can't be less than fifteen, for I met her in 1966.
But she was a treasure even then, and the man I bought her
from cheated himself horribly. He was getting married *much*
too quickly and needed folding money in a hurry. All I can
say is, I hope he got one hell of a wife—because I sure
got one hell of a guitar.

She's a J-45, red sunburst with a custom neck, and she
clearly predates the Great Guitar Boom of the Sixties. She
is *hand-made,* not machine-stamped, and she is some forgotten artisan's masterpiece. The very best, top-of-the-line
Gibson made today could not touch her; there are very few
guitars you can buy that would. She has been my other
voice and the basic tool of my trade for a decade and a half.
Now her neck, and my heart, were broken clean through.

Long-Drink McGonnigle was at my side, looking mournfully down past me at the pitiful thing on the bar. He touched
one of the sprawled strings. It rattled. Death rattle. "Aw,"
he murmured.

Callahan put a triple Bushmill's in my hand, closed my
fingers around it. I made it a double, and then I turned and
walked to the chalk line on the floor, faced the merrily
crackling fireplace from a distance of twenty feet. People
waited respectfully. I drank again while I considered my
toast. Then I raised my glass, and everybody followed suit.

"To the Lady," I said, and drained my glass and threw
it at the back of the fireplace, and then I said, "Sorry, folks,"
because it's very difficult to make Mike's fireplace emit
shards of glass—it's designed like a parabolic reflector with
a shallow focus—but I had thrown hard enough to spatter
four tables just the same. I know better than to throw that
hard.

Nobody paid the least mind; as one they chorused, "To the Lady" and drank, and when the barrage was finished, *eight* tables were littered with shards.

Then there was a pause, while everybody waited to see if I could talk about it yet. The certain knowledge that they were prepared to swallow their curiosity, go back to their drinking and ignore me if that were what I needed, made it possible to speak.

"I was coming offstage. The Purple Cat, over in East-hampton. Tripped over a cable in the dark. Knew I was going down, tried to get her out from under me. The stage there is waist-high, her head just cleared it and wedged in under the monitor speaker. Then my weight came down on her..." I was sobbing. "...and she *screamed*, and I..."

Long-Drink wrapped me in his great long arms and hugged tight. I buried my face in his shirt and wept. Someone else hugged us both from behind me. When I was back under control, both let go and I found a drink in my hand. I gulped it gratefully.

"I hate to ask, Jake," Callahan rumbled. "I'm afraid I already know. Is there any chance she could be fixed?"

"Tell him, Eddie." But Eddie wasn't there; his piano stool was empty. "All right, look, Mike: There are probably ten shops right here on Long Island that'd accept the commission and my money, and maybe an equal number who'd be honest enough to turn me away. There are maybe five real guitar-makers in the whole New York area, and they'd all tell me to forget it. There might be four Master-class artisans still alive in all of North America, and their bill would run to four figures, maybe five, assuming they thought they could save her at all." Noah Gonzalez had removed his hat, with a view toward passing it; he put it back on. "*Look at her.* You can't *get* wood like that anymore. She's got a custom neck and fingerboard, skinnier'n usual, puts the strings closer together—when I play a normal guitar it's like my fingers shrunk. So a rebuilt neck would have less strength, and the fingerboard'd have to be hand-made..." I stopped myself. I finished my drink. "Mike, she's dead."

Long-Drink burst into tears. Callahan nodded and looked

sad, and passed me another big drink. He poured one for himself, and *he* toasted the Lady, and when that barrage was over he set 'em up for the house.

The folks treated me right; we had a proper Irish wake for the Lady, and it got pretty drunk out. We laughed and danced and reminisced and swapped lies, created grand toasts; everyone did it up nice. The only thing it lacked was Eddie on the piano; he had disappeared and none knew where. But a wake for Lady Macbeth *must* include the voice of her long-time colleague—so Callahan surprised us all by sitting down and turning out some creditable barrelhouse. I hadn't known he could play a note, and I'd have sworn his fingers were too big to hit only one key at a time, but he did okay.

Anyhow, when the smoke cleared, Pyotr ended up driving better than half of us home, in groups of three—a task I wouldn't wish on my senator.

I guess I should explain about Pyotr. . . .

The thing about a joint like Callahan's Place is that it could not possibly function without the cooperation of all its patrons. It takes a lot of volunteer effort to make the Place work the way it does.

Some of this is obvious. Clearly, if a barkeep is going to allow his patrons to smash their empties in the fireplace, they must all be responsible enough to exercise prudence in this pursuit—and furthermore they must have better than average aim. But perhaps it is not obvious, and so I should mention, that there is a broom-and-scoop set on either side of the hearth, and whenever an occasional wild shard ricochets across the room, one of those broom-and-scoops just naturally finds its way into the hands of whoever happens to be nearest, without anything being said.

Similarly, if you like a parking lot in which anarchy reigns, with cars parked every which way like goats in a pen, you must all be prepared to pile outside together six or ten times a night, and back-and-fill in series until whoever is trying to leave can get his car out. This recurring scene looks rather like a grand-scale Chinese Fire Drill, or perhaps like Bumper Cars for Grownups; Doc Webster points out that to a Martian it would probably look like some vast robot orgy, and insists on referring to it as Auto-Eroticism.

Then there's closing ritual. Along about fifteen minutes before closing, somebody, usually Fast Eddie Costigan the piano player, comes around to all the tables with a big plastic-lined trash barrel. Each table has one of those funnel-and-tin-can ashtrays; someone at each table unscrews it and dumps the butts into the barrel. Then Eddie inserts two corners of the plastic tablecloth into the barrel, the customer lifts the other two corners into the air, and Eddie sluices off the cloth with a seltzer bottle. Other cleanup jobs, mopping and straight-ening and the like, just seem to get done by somebody or other every night; all Mike Callahan ever had to do is polish the bartop, turn out the lights and go home. Consequently, al-though he is scrupulous about ceasing to sell booze at legal curfew, Mike is in no hurry to chase his friends out, and indeed I know of several occasions on which he kept the Place open round the clock, giving away nosepaint until the hour arrived at which it became legal to sell it again.

And finally, of course, there's old Pyotr. You see, no one tight drives home from Callahan's bar. When Mike decides that you've had enough—and they'll never make a Breathalyzer as accurate as his professional judgment—the only way in the world you will get another drink from him is to surrender your car keys and then let Pyotr, who drinks only distilled water, drive you home when you fold. The next morning you drive Pyotr back to his cottage, which is just up the street from Callahan's, and if this seems like too much trouble, you can always go drink somewhere else and see what that gets you.

For the first couple of years after Pyotr started coming around, some of us used to wonder what he got out of the arrangement. None of us ever managed to get him to accept so much as a free breakfast the morning after, and how do you buy a drink for a man who drinks distilled water? Oh, Mike gave him the water for free, but a gallon or so of water a night is pretty poor wages for all the hours of driving Pyotr put in, in the company of at least occasionally troublesome drunks, not to mention the inconvenience of spending many nights sleeping on a strange bed or couch or floor. (Some of the boys, and especially the ones who want to get pie-eyed once in a while, are married. Almost to a woman, their wives worship Pyotr; are happy to put him up now and then.)

For that matter, none of us could ever figure out what old Pyotr did for a living. He never had to be anywhere at any particular time next morning, and he was never late arriving at Callahan's. If asked what he did he would say, "Oh, a little bit of everything, whenever I can get it," and drop the subject. Yet he never seemed to be in need of money, and in all the time I knew him I never once saw him take so much as a peanut from the Free Lunch.

(In Callahan's Place there *is* a free lunch—supported by donations. The value of the change in the jar is almost always greater than the value of the Free Lunch next to it, but nobody watches to make sure it stays that way. I mind me of a bad two weeks when that Free Lunch was the only protein I had, and nobody so much as frowned at me.)

But while he is a bit on the pale side for a man of Middle European stock, Pyotr certainly never looks undernourished, and so there was never any need for us to pry into his personal affairs. Me, I figured him for some kind of a pensioner with a streak of pure altruism, and let it go.

He certainly looks old enough to be a pensioner. Oh, he's in very good shape for his age, and not overly afflicted with wrinkles, but his complexion has that old-leather look. And when you notice his habit of speaking into his cupped hand, and hear the slight lisp in his speech, and you realize that his smiles never seem to pry his lips apart, you get the idea that he's missing some bridgework. And there's something old about his eyes. . . .

Anyway, Pyotr was busier than usual that night, ferrying home all the casualties of Lady Macbeth's wake. It took quite a while. He took three at a time, using the vehicle of whoever lived furthest away, and taxied back for the next load. Two out of every three drunks would have to taxi back to Callahan's the next day for their cars. I was proud of the honor being paid my dead Lady. Pyotr and Callahan decided to save me for last. Perhaps on the principle that the worst should come last—I was *pissed,* and at the stage of being offensively cheerful and hearty. At last all the other wounded had been choppered out, and Pyotr tapped me on one weaving shoulder.

"So they weld—well hell, hi, Pyotr, wait a half while I finish telling Mike this story—they weld manacles on this giant alien, and they haul him into court for trial, and the first thing he does, they go to swear him in and he swallows the bailiff whole."

Mike had told *me* this gag, but he is a very compassionate man. He relit his cheroot and gave me the straight line, "What'd the bailiff do?"

"His job, o'course—he swore, in the witness. Haw haw!" Pyotr joined in the polite laughter and took my arm. "Time to bottle it up, Pyotr you old lovable Litvak? Time to scamper, is it? Why should you have to haul my old ashes, huh? Gimme my keys, Mike, I'm not nearly so drunk as you think—I mean, so thunk as you drink. Shit, I said it right, I *must* be drink. All right, just let me find my pants—"

It took both of them to get me to the car. I noticed that every time one of my feet came unstuck from the ground, it seemed to take enormous effort to force it back down again. A car seat leaped up and hit me in the ass, and a door slammed. "Make sure he takes two aspirins before he passes out for good," Callahan's voice said from a mile away.

"Right," Pyotr said from only a few blocks distant, and my old Pontiac woke up grumbling. The world lurched suddenly, and we fell off a cliff, landing a million years later in white water. I felt nausea coming on, chattered merrily to stave it off.

"Splendid business, Pyotr old sock, absolutionally magnelephant. You drive well, and this car handles well on ice, but if you keep spinning like this we're going to dend up in the itch—mean, we'll rote off the ride, right? Let's go to the Brooklyn Navy Yard and try to buy a drink for every sailor on the *U.S.S. Missouri*—as a songwriter I'm always hoping to find the Moe juiced. Left her right there on the bartop, by all the gods! Jus' left her and—turn around, God damn it, I left my Lady back there!"

"It is all right, Jake. Mr. Callahan will leave her locked up. We will wake her for several days, correct Irish custom, yes? Even those not present tonight should have opportunity to pay their respects."

"Hell, yeah, sure. Hey! *Funeral*. How? Bury or cremate?"

"Cremation would seem appropriate."

"*Strings?* Gearboxes? Heavy metal air pollution? Fuggoff. Bury her, dissolve in acid, heave her into the ocean off Montauk Point and let the fish lay eggs in her sounding box. Know why I called her Lady Macbeth?"

"No, I never knew."

"Used to sneak up and stab me inna back when didn't expect it. Bust a string, go out of tune, start to buzz on the high frets for no reason at all. Treacherous bitch. Oh, *Lady!*"

"You used each other well, Jake. Be glad. Not many have ever touched so fine an instrument."

"Goddam right. Stop the car, please. I want to review inputs."

"Open the window."

"I'll get it all over the—"

"It's raining. Go ahead."

"Oh. Not sure I like Finn's magic. Have to pay attention to notice it's raining. Right ho. *Oh.*"

Eventually the car stopped complaining and rain sprinkled everything but Pyotr and me and then my house opened up and swallowed me. "Forget aspirins," I mumbled as my bed rushed at me. "Don' need 'em."

"You'll be sorry tomorrow."

"I'm sorry now."

The bed and I went inertialess together, spun end over end across the macrocosmic Universe.

I was awakened by the deafening thunder of my pulse.

I knew that I was awake long before I had the power to raise my eyelids. I knew it because I knew I lacked the imagination to dream a taste like that in my mouth. But I was quite prepared to believe that the sleep had lasted at least a century; I felt *old*. That made me wonder if I had snored right through the wake—*the wake!* Everything came back in a rush; I flung open my eyes, and two large icicles were rammed into the apertures as far as they would go, the points inches deep in my forebrain. I screamed. That is, I tried to scream, and it sounded like a scream—but my pulse sounded like an empty oil tank being hit with a maul, so more likely what I did was bleat or whimper.

Something heavy and bristly lay across me; it felt like horsehair, with the horse still attached. I strained at it, could not budge it. I wept.

The voice spoke in an earsplitting whisper. "Good morning, Jake."

"Fuck you too," I croaked savagely, wincing as the smell of my breath went past my nose.

"I warned you," Pyotr said sadly.

"Fuck you twice. Jesus, my eyelashes hurt. What is *lying* on me?"

"A cotton sheet."

"Gaah."

"You should have accepted the aspirins."

"You don't understand. I don't get hangovers."

Pyotr made no reply.

"Damn it, I don't! Not even when I was a lush, not the first time I ever got smashed, not *ever*. Trick metabolism. Worst that ever happens is I wake up not hungry—but no head, no nausea, no weakness, never."

Pyotr was silent a long time. Then, "You drank a good deal more than usual last night."

"Hell, I been drunker'n *that*. Too many times, man."

"Never since I have known you."

"Well, that's true. Maybe that's . . . no, I've fallen off the wagon before. I just don't get hangovers."

He left the room, was gone awhile. I passed the time working on a comprehensive catalog of all the places that hurt, beginning with my thumbnails. I got quite a lot of work done before Pyotr returned; I had gotten halfway through the hairs on my forearms when he came in the door with a heavily laden tray in his hands. I opened my mouth to scream, "Get that *food* out of here!"—and the smell reached me. I sat up and began to salivate. He set the tray down on my lap and I ignored the pain and annihilated bacon, sausage, eggs, cheese, onions, green peppers, hot peppers, bread, butter, English muffins, jam, orange juice, coffee, and assorted condiments so fast I think I frightened him a little. When I sank back against the pillows the tray contained a plate licked clean, an empty cup and glass, and a fork. I was exhausted, and still hurt in all the same places— that is, in all places—but I was beginning to believe that I wanted to live. "This is crazy," I said. "If I *am* hung over, the concept of food ought to be obscene. I never ate that much breakfast in my life, not even the morning after my wedding night."

I could *see* Pyotr now, and he looked embarrassed, as though my appetite were his fault.

"What time is it?"

"Seven P.M."

"God's teeth."

"It was four in the morning when we arrived here. You have slept for thirteen hours. I fell asleep at noon and have just awakened. Do you feel better now that you have eaten?"

"No, but I concede the trick is possible. What's good for total bodily agony?"

"Well, there is no cure. But certain medications are said to alleviate the symptoms."

"And Callahan's has opened by now. Well, how do we get me to the car?"

•   •   •

In due course we got to Callahan's where Lady Macbeth lay in state on top of the bar. The wake was already in full swing when we arrived and were greeted with tipsy cheers. I saw that it was Riddle Night: The big blackboard stood near the door, tonight's game scrawled on it in the handwriting of Doc Webster. On Riddle Night the previous week's winner is Riddle Master; each solved riddle is good for a drink on the Riddle Master's tab. The Doc looked fairly happy—every *un*solved riddle is a free drink for him, on the house.

The board was headed "PUBLIC PERSONALITIES." Beneath that were inscribed the following runes:

I.

a) Hindu ascetic; masculine profession
b) tramp; crane
c) profligate; cheat
d) span; tavern, money
e) fish; Jamaican or Scottish male, caviar
f) certainly; Irish street
g) handtruck; forgiveness

II.

a) pry; manager
b) smart guy; Stout
c) chicken coop; more loving
d) bandit; crimson car
e) coffin; baby boy
f) tote; subsidy
g) moaning; achieve

III.

a) irrigated; laser pistol
b) Nazi; cook lightly
c) British punk; knowledge, current
d) chicken coop; foreplay
e) wealthier; nuts to

IV.
   a)   Italian beauty; stead, depart, witness
   b)   toilet; auto, senior member
   c)   be dull; Carmina Burana
   d)   grass; apprentice, younger
   e)   valley; odd
   f)   burns; leer at

Example: penis; truck = peter; lorry = Peter
Lorre. Extra drinks for identifying Categories
I-IV.

People were staring at the board, seemed to have *been*
staring at it for some time, but none of the riddles were
checked off yet. I paid my respects to the Lady, said hello
to Mike, accepted a large glass of dog-hair. Then, deliberately, I turned away from the Lady and toward the board.
(Why don't you take a crack at it before reading further?)

"Got one," I said at once, and allowed Long-Drink to
help me to the board. "First one in line," I said, marking
with chalk. "Hindu ascetic; masculine profession. That's
Jain; Man's Field, and Category One is Actresses."

Doc Webster looked pained. "Say Film Women," he sug-
gested. "More accurate. Mike, one for Jake on me."

Given the category Section I was fairly simple. I got b)
'Bo; Derrick. Long-Drink McGonnigle got c) Rakehell;
Welsh. Tommy Janssen figured out that d) and e) were
Bridge It; Bar Dough and Marlin; Mon Roe. Josie Bauer
took f) Surely; Mick Lane and g) Dolly; Pardon. We col-
lected our drinks gleefully.

I suspected that the second category would be Male Ac-
tors (or Film Men), but kept my mouth shut, hoping I could
figure them all out and do a sweep before anyone else
twigged. This turned out to be poor tactics; I got a), b), d)
and f), but while I was puzzling over the rest, Shorty Steinitz
spoke up. "The category is Male Film Stars, and the first
one is Jimmy; Steward!" I tried to jump in at once, but
Long-Drink drowned me out. "Got b): Alec; Guinness! Hey,
and f) has to be Carry; Grant."

"And d)," I said irritably, "is Robber; Red Ford. But what about the others?" We stared at them in silence for awhile.

"A hint," Doc Webster said at last. "With reference to g), the first name is what I'll be doing if you do the second."

"Got it!" Long-Drink cried. "Keenin'; Win." The Doc grimaced. Callahan was busy keeping score and distributing the prizes, but he had attention left to spare. "That third one there, c): That has to be Hennery; Fonder."

There was a pause, then. Nobody could figure out "coffin; baby boy." (Can you?) After awhile we turned our attention to the remaining two categories, but the silence remained unbroken. The Doc looked smug. "No hurry, gents and ladies," he said. "Closing time isn't for several hours yet." We all glared at him and thought hard.

Surprisingly, it was Pyotr who spoke up. "I have a sweep," he stated. "Category IV in its entirety."

Folks regarded him with respectful interest. He was committed now: if he missed *one,* he would owe the Doc all six drinks. The Doc looked startled but game—he seemed to think he had an ace up his sleeve. "Go ahead, Pyotr."

"The category is Famous Monsters." The Doc winced. "The first is Bella; Lieu Go See." Applause. "Then John; Car a Dean." More applause.

"Not bad," the Doc admitted. "Keep going."

"The next two, of course, are among the most famous of all. Be dull; Carmina Burana *has* to be Bore Us; Carl Orff. . . ." He paused to sip one of the three drinks Callahan had passed him.

"Brilliant, Pyotr," I said, slapping him on the back. "But I'm still stumped for the last three."

"That is because they are tricky. The first is tortured, and the last two are obscure."

"Go ahead," Doc Webster said grimly.

"The first is the famous Wolfman: Lawn; Trainee Junior." Delighted laughter and applause came from all sides. "The others are both Frankenstein's Creature, but it would require an historian of horror films to guess both. Glenn Strange played the Monster in at least three movies..." The Doc swore. "... and the last shall be first; the man who played the Monster in the very first film version of *Frankenstein*."

"But we already had Karloff," I protested.

"No, Jake," Pyotr said patiently. "That was the first *talkie* version. The very first was released in 1910, and the Monster was played by a man with the unusual name of Charles Ogle. Read 'chars' for 'burns' and you come close enough."

We gave him a standing ovation—in which the Doc joined.

All of this had admirably occupied my attention, from almost the moment of my arrival. But before I turned to a study of Category III, I turned to the bar to begin the third of the four drinks I had won—and my gaze fell on the ruined Lady. She lay there in tragic splendor, mutely reproaching me for enjoying myself so much while she was broken. All at once I lost all interest in the game, in everything but the pressing business of locating and obtaining oblivion. I gulped the drink in my hand and reached for the next one, and a very elderly man came in the door of Callahan's Place with his hands high in the air, an expression of infinite weariness on his face. He was closely followed by Fast Eddie Costigan, whose head just about came up to the level of the elderly man's shoulder blades. Conversations began to peter out.

I just had time to recall that Eddie had vanished mysteriously the night before, and then the two of them moved closer and I saw why everybody was getting quiet. And why the old gent had his hands in the air. I didn't get a real good look, but what Eddie had in his right hand, nestled up against the other man's fourth lumbar vertebra, looked an awful lot like a Charter Arms .38. The gun that got Johnny Lennon and George Wallace.

I decided which way I would jump and put on my blandest expression. "Hi, Eddie."

"Hi, Jake," he said shortly, all his attention on his prisoner.

"I tell you for the last time, Edward—," the old gent began in a Spanish accent.

"Shaddap! Nobody ast you nuttin'. Get over here by de bar an' get to it, see?"

"Eddie," Callahan began gently.

"Shaddap, I said."

I was shocked. Eddie *worships* Callahan. The runty little piano man prodded with his piece, and the old Spaniard sighed in resignation and came toward me.

But as he came past me, his expression changed suddenly and utterly. If aged Odysseus had come round one last weary corner and found Penelope in a bower, legs spread and a sweet smile on her lips, his face might have gone through such a change. The old gent was staring past me in joyous disbelief at the Holy Grail, at the Golden Fleece, at the Promised Land, at—

—at the ruined Lady Macbeth.

"Santa Maria," he breathed. *"Madre de Dios."*

Years lifted from his shoulders, bitter years, and years smoothed away from his face. His hands came down slowly to his sides, and I saw those hands, really *saw* them for the first time. All at once I knew who he was. My eyes widened.

"Montoya," I said. "Domingo Montoya."

He nodded absently.

"But you're dead."

He nodded again, and moved forward. His eyes were dreamy, but his step was firm. Eddie stood his ground. Montoya stopped before the Lady, and he actually bowed to her. And then he looked at her.

First he let his eyes travel up her length the way a man takes in a woman, from the toes up. I watched his face. He almost smiled when he reached the bridge. He almost frowned when he got to the scars around the sounding hole that said I had once been foolish enough to clamp a pick-up onto her. He did smile as his gaze reached the fingerboard and frets, and he marveled at the lines of the neck. Then his eyes reached the awful fracture, and they shut for an instant. His face became totally expressionless; his eyes opened again, studied the wreck with dispassionate thoroughness, and went on to study the head.

That first look took him perhaps eight seconds. He straightened up, closed his eyes again, clearly fixing the memory forever in his brain. Then he turned to me. "Thank you, sir," he said with great formality. "You are a very fortunate man."

I thought about it. "Yes, I believe I am."

He turned back and looked at her again, and now he *looked*. From several angles, from up close and far away. The joining of neck to body. The joining of head to neck-stub. "Light," he said, and held out his hand. Callahan put a flashlight into it, and Montoya inspected what he could of Lady Macbeth's interior bracings through her open mouth. I had the damndest feeling that he was going to tell her to stick out her tongue and say "Ah!" He tossed the flashlight over his shoulder—Eddie caught it with his free hand—and stooped to sight along the neck. "Towel," he said, straightening. Callahan produced a clean one. He wiped his hands very carefully, finger by finger, and then with the tenderness of a mother bathing her child he began to touch the Lady here and there.

"Jake," Long-Drink said in hushed tones. "What the hell is going on? Who *is* this guy?"

Montoya gave no sign of hearing; he was absorbed.

"Remember what I said last night? That there are only maybe four Master-class guitar makers left in the country?"

"Yeah. This guy's a Master?"

"No," I cried, scandalized.

"Well then?"

"There is one rank higher than Master. Wizard. There have been a dozen or so in all the history of the world. Domingo Montoya is the only one now living." I gulped Irish whiskey. "Except that he died five years ago."

"The hell you say."

Fast Eddie stuffed the gun into his belt and sat down on his piano stool. "He didn't die," he said, signalling Callahan for a rum. "He went underground."

I nodded. "I think I understand."

Long-Drink shook his head. "I don't."

"Okay, Drink, think about it a second. Put yourself in his shoes. You're Domingo Montoya, the last living guitar Wizard. *And all they bring you to work on is shit.* There are maybe fifty or a hundred guitars left on the planet worthy of your skill, most of which you made yourself, and they're all being *well* cared for by careful and wealthy owners. Meanwhile, fools keep coming in the door with their broken toys, their machine-stamped trash, asking Paul Dirac to do their physics homework for them. Damnfool Marquises who want a guitar with the name of their mistress spelled out in jewels on the neck; idiot rock stars who want a guitar shaped like a Swiss Army knife; stupid rich kids who want their stupid Martins and stupid Goyas outfitted with day-glo pick-guards by the man everyone knows is the last living Wizard. Nobody wants to pay what honest materials cost nowadays, nobody wants to wait as long as true Quality requires, every-body wants their goddamn lily gilded, and *still* you can't beat them off with a club, because you're Domingo Mon-toya. You triple your fee, and then triple it again, and then square the result, and still they keep coming with their stupid broken trash—or worse, they purchase one of your own handmade masterworks, and use it ignobly, fail to respect it properly, treat it like some sort of common utensil." I glanced at Montoya. "No wonder he retired."

Montoya looked up. "I have not retired. If God is kind I never will. But I no longer sell my skill or its fruits, and I use another name. I did not believe it was possible to locate me."

"Then how—"

"Two years ago I accepted an apprentice." My brows went up; I would not have thought there was anyone worthy to be the pupil of Domingo Montoya. "He is impatient and lacks serenity, but both of these are curable with age. He is not clumsy, and his attitude is good." He glowered at Eddie. *"Was* good. He swore secrecy to me."

"I went ta school wit' 'im," Eddie said. "P.S. Eighty-t'ree. He hadda tell *some*body."

"Yes," Montoya said, nodding slowly. "I suppose I can see how that would be so."

"He come back ta de old neighborhood ta see his Ma. I run into 'im on de street an' we go to a gin mill an' pretty soon he's tellin' me de whole story, how he's never been so happy in his life. He tells me ta come out to Ohio an' meetcha sometime, an' he gimme yer address." Eddie glanced down at the gun in his belt and looked sheepish. "I guess he sh'unta done dat."

Montoya looked at him, and then at Lady Macbeth, and then at me. He looked me over very carefully, and to my great relief I passed muster. "No harm done," he said to Eddie, and for the first time I noticed that Montoya was wearing a sweater, pajamas, and bedroom slippers.

I was bursting with the need to ask, and I *could not ask*, I was afraid to ask, and it must have showed in my face, at least to a gaze as piercing as his, because all of a sudden his own face got all remorseful and compassionate. My heart sank. It was beyond even his skill—

"Forgive me, sir," he said mournfully. "I have kept you waiting for my prognosis. I am old, my mind is full of fur. I will take you, how is it said, off the tender hooks."

I finished my drink in a swallow, lobbed the empty into the fireplace for luck, and gripped both arms of my chair. "Shoot."

"You do not want to know, can this guitar be mended. This is not at issue. You know that any imbecile can butt the two ends together and brace and glue and tinker and give you back something which looks just like a guitar. What you want to know is, can this guitar ever be what she was two days ago, and I tell you the answer is never in this world."

I closed my eyes and inhaled sharply; all the tiny various outposts of hangover throughout my body rose up and *throbbed* all at once.

Montoya was still speaking. "—trauma so great as this must have subtle effects all throughout the instrument, microscopic ruptures, tiny weakenings. No man could trace them all, nor heal them if he did. But if you ask me can I, Domingo Montoya, make this guitar so *close* to what it was that you yourself cannot detect any difference, then I tell you that I believe I can; also I can fix that buzz I see in the twelfth fret and replace your pegs."

My ears roared.

"I cannot guarantee success! But I believe I can do it. At worst I will have to redesign the head. It will take me two months. For that period I will loan you one of my guitars. You must keep your hands in shape for her, while she is healing for you. You have treated her with kindness, I can see; she will not malinger."

I could not speak. It was Callahan who said, "What is your fee, Don Domingo?"

He shook his head. "There is no charge. My eyes and hands tell me that this guitar was made by an old pupil of mine, Goldman. He went to work for Gibson, and then he saw the way the industry was going and got into another line. I always thought that if he had kept working, kept learning, he might have taught me one day." He caressed the guitar. "It is good to see his handiwork. I *want* to mend her. How daring the neck! She must be a pleasure to play once you are used to her, eh?"

"She is. Thank you, Don Domingo."

"Nobody here will reveal your secret," Callahan added. "Oh, and say, I've got a jug of fine old Spanish wine in the back I been saving for a gentleman such as yourself—could I pour you a glass on the house? Maybe a sandwich to go with it?"

Montoya smiled.

I swiveled my chair away from him. *"Eddie!"* I cried.

The little piano man read my expression, and his eyes widened in shock and horror. "Aw Jeez," he said, shaking his head, "aw, *naw,"* and I left my chair like a stone leaving a slingshot. Eddie bolted for cover, but strong volunteers grabbed him and prevented his escape. I was on him like a stooping falcon, wrapping him up in my arms and kissing him on the mouth before he could turn his face away. An explosion of laughter and cheers shook the room, and he turned bright red. "Aw *Jeez!*" he said again.

"Eddie," I cried, "there is no way I will *ever* be able to repay you."

"Sure dere is," he yelled. "Leggo o' me."

More laughter and cheers. Then Doc Webster spoke up.

"Eddie, that was a good thing you did, and I love you for it. And I know you tend to use direct methods, and I can't argue with results. But frankly I'm a little disappointed to learn that you own a handgun."

"I bought it on de way to Ohio," Eddie said, struggling free of my embrace. "I figger maybe de Wizard don' wanna get up at seven inna mornin' an' drive five hunnert miles to look at no busted axe. Sure enough, he don't."

"But dammit, Eddie, those things are dangerous. Over the course of a five-hundred-mile drive . . . suppose he tried to get that gun away from you, and it went off?"

Eddie pulled the gun, aimed it at the ceiling, and pulled the trigger. There was no explosion. Only a small clacking sound as the hammer fell and then an inexplicable loud hiss. Eddie rotated the cylinder slightly. In a loud voice with too much treble, the gun offered to clear up my pimples overnight without messy creams or oily pads.

It actually had time to finish its pitch, give the time and call-letters, and begin Number Three on the Hot Line of Hits before the tidal wave of laughter and applause drowned it out. Montoya left off soothing the wounded Lady to join in, and when he could make himself heard, he called, "You could have threatened me with nothing more fearsome, my friend, than forced exposure to AM radio," at which Eddie broke up and flung the "gun" into the fireplace.

Eventually it got worked out that Eddie and Montoya would bring Lady Macbeth back to Eddie's place together, get some sleep, and set out the next morning for Montoya's home, where he could begin work. Eddie would bring me back the promised loaner, would be back with it by the night after next, and on his return we would jam together. Montoya made me promise to tape that jam and send him a dupe.

What with one thing and another, I finished up that evening just about as pickled as I'd been the night before. But it was happy drunk rather than sad drunk, an altogether different experience, in kind if not in degree. Popular myth to the contrary, drink is not really a good drug for pain. That is, it can numb physical pain, but will not blunt the edge of sorrow; it can help that latter only by making it easier for a man to curse or weep. But alcohol is great for happiness: it can actually intensify joy. It was perfect for the occasion, then; it anesthetized me against the unaccustomed aches of my first hangover, and enhanced my euphoria. My Lady was saved, she would sing again. My friends, who had shared my loss, shared my joy. I danced with Josie and Eddie and Rachel and Leslie; I solved Category III of Doc's riddle and swept it without a mistake; I jollied Tommy out of being worried about some old friend of his, and made him laugh; with Eddie on piano and everybody else in the joint as the Raelettes I sang "What'd I Say" for seventeen choruses; for at least half an hour I studied the grain on the bartop and learned therefrom a great deal about the structure and purpose of the Universe; I leaped up on the same bartop and performed a hornpipe—on my hands. After that it all got a bit vague and hallucinatory— at least, I don't *think* there were any real horses present.

A short while later it seemed to be unusually quiet. The only sound was the steady cursing of my Pontiac and the hissing of the air that it sliced through. I opened my eyes and watched white lines come at me.

"Pyotr. Stout fellow. No—water fellow, won't drink stout. Why don't you drink, Pyotr? S'*nice*."

"Weak stomach. Rest, Jake. Soon we are home."

"Hope I'm not hung over again tomorrow. That was awful. Cripes, my neck still hurts...." I started to rub it; Pyotr took my hand away.

"Leave it alone, Jake. Rest. Tonight I will make sure you take two aspirins."

"Yeah. You're the lily of the valley, man."

A short while later wetness occurred within my mouth in alarming proportions, and when I swallowed I felt the aspirins going down. "Good old Pyotr." Then the ship's engines shut down and we went into free fall.

Next morning I decided that hangovers are like sex— the second time isn't *quite* as painful. If the analogy held, by tomorrow I'd be enjoying it.

Oh, I hurt, all right. No mistake about that. But I hurt like a man with a medium bad case of the flu, whereas the day before I had hurt like a man systematically tortured for information over a period of weeks. This time sensory stimuli were only about twice the intensity I could handle, and a considerably younger and smaller mouse had died in my mouth, and my skull was no more than a half size too small. The only thing that hurt as much as it had the previous morning was my neck, as I learned when I made an ill-advised attempt to consult the clock beside me on the night table. For a horrified moment I actually *believed* that I had unscrewed my skull and now it was falling off. I put it back on with my hands, and it felt like I nearly stripped the threads until I got it right.

I must have emitted sound. The door opened and Pyotr looked in. "Are you all right, Jake?"

"Of course not—half of me is left. Saved me for last again, eh?"

"You insisted. In fact you could not be persuaded to leave at all, until you lost consciousness altogether."

"Well, I—OH! *My guitar.* Oh, Pyotr, I think I'm going to do something that will hurt me very much."

"What?"

"I am going to smile."

It did hurt. If you don't happen to be hung over, relax your face and put a finger just behind and beneath each ear, and concentrate. Now smile. The back of my neck was a knot of pain, and those two muscles you just felt move were the ends of the knot. Smiling tightened it. But I had to smile, and didn't mind the pain. Lady Macbeth was alive! Life was good.

That didn't last; my metabolism just wasn't up to supporting good cheer. The Lady was *not* alive. Back from the dead, perhaps—but still in deep coma in Intensive Care. Attended, to be sure, by the world's best surgeon. But she did not have youth going for her—and neither did the surgeon.

Pyotr must have seen the smile fade and guessed why, because he said exactly the right thing.

"There is hope, my friend."

I took my first real good look at him.

"Thanks, Pyotr. Gawd, you look worse than I do. I must have woken you up, what time is it, I don't dare turn my head and look."

"Much like yesterday. You have slept the clock 'round, and I have just finished my customary six hours. I admit I do not feel very rested."

"You must be coming down with something. Truly, man, you look like I feel."

"How *do* you feel?"

"Uh—oddly enough, not as bad as I expected to. Those aspirins must have helped. Thanks, brother."

He ducked his head in what I took to be modesty or shyness.

"You should take a couple yourself."

He shook his head. "I am one of those people who can't take asp—"

"No problem, I've got the other kind, good for all stomachs."

"Thank you, no."

"You sure? What time did you say it was?"

"Normal people are eating their dinners."

"Their—*dinner!*" I sat up, ignoring all agony, got to my feet and staggered headlong out of the room, down the hall to the kitchen. I wept with joy at the sight of so much food in one place. That same eerie, voracious hunger of the morning before, except that today I was not going to make Pyotr do the cooking. I was ashamed enough to note that he had cleaned up the previous night's breakner (a compound word formed along the same lines as "brunch"), apparently before he had gone to sleep.

I designed a megaomelet and began amassing construction materials. I designed for twin occupants. "Pyotr, you old Slovak Samaritan, I know you have this thing about not letting people stand you to a meal the next day, and I can dig that, makes the generosity more pure, but I've been with you now close to forty hours and you've had bugger all to eat, so what you're gonna do is sit down and shut up and eat this omelet or I'm gonna shove it up your nose, right?"

He stared in horror at the growing pile on the cutting board. "Jake, no, thank you! No."

"Well, God damn it, Pyotr, I ain't asking for a structural analysis of your digestion! Just tell me what ingredients to leave out and I'll double up on the rest."

"No, truly—"

"Damn it, anybody can eat *eggs*."

"Jake, thank you, I truly am not at all hungry."

I gave up. By that time all eight eggs had already been cracked, so I cut enough other things to fill an eight-egg omelet anyhow, figuring I'd give the other half to the cats. But to my surprise, when I paused to wipe my mouth, there was nothing left before me that I could legitimately eat except for a piece of ham gristle I had rejected once already. So I ate it, and finished the pot of coffee, and looked up.

"Cripes, maybe you really are sick. I'm gonna call Doc Webster—"

"Thank you, no, Jake, I would appreciate only a ride home, if you please, and to lie down and rest. If you are up to it. . . ."

"Hell, I feel practically vertebrate. Only thing still sore is the back of my neck. Just let me shower and change and we'll hit the road."

I pulled up in front of Pyotr's place, a small dark cottage

all by itself about a half a block from Callahan's Place. I got out with him. "I'll just come in with you for a second, Pyotr, get you squared away."

"You are kind to offer, but I am fine now. I will sleep tonight, and see you tomorrow. Goodbye, Jake—I am glad your guitar is not lost."

So I got back into the car and drove the half block to Callahan's.

"Evenin', Jake. What'll it be?"

"Coffee, please, light and sweet."

Callahan nodded approvingly. "Coming up."

Long-Drink snorted next to me. "Can't take the gaff, huh, youngster?"

"I guess not, Drink. These last two mornings I've had the first two hangovers of my life. I guess I'm getting old."

"Hah!" The Drink looked suddenly puzzled. "You know, now I come to think of it . . . huh. I never thought."

"And no one ever accused you of it, either."

"No, I mean I just now come to realize what a blessed long time it's been since I been hung over myself."

"Really? You?" The Drink is one of Pyotr's steadiest (or unsteadiest) customers. "You must have the same funny metabolism I have—ouch!" I rubbed the back of my neck. "Used to have."

"No," he said thoughtfully. "No, I've *had* hangovers. Lots of 'em. Only I just realized I can't remember when was the last *time* I had one."

Slippery Joe Maser had overheard. "I can. Remember *my* last hangover, I mean. About four years ago. Just before I started comin' here. Boy, it was a honey—"

"Ain't that funny?" Noah Gonzalez put in. "Damned if I can remember a hangover since I started drinking here myself. Used to get 'em all the time. I sort of figured it had something to do with the vibes in this joint."

Joe nodded. "That's what I thought. This Place is kinda magic, everybody knows that. Boy, I always wake up hungry after a toot, though. Hell of a stiff neck, too."

"Magic, hell," Long-Drink said. "Callahan, you thievin' spalpeen, we've got you red-handed! Waterin' your drinks, by God, not an honest hangover in a hogshead. Admit it."

"I'll admit you got a hog's head, all right," Callahan growled back, returning with my coffee. He stuck his seven o'clock shadow an inch from Long-Drink's and exhaled rancorous cigar smoke. "If my booze is watered down, how the hell come it gets you so damn pie-faced?"

"Power of suggestion," the Drink roared. "Placebo effect. Contact high from these other rummies. Tell him, Doc."

Doc Webster, who had been sitting quietly hunched over his drink, chose this moment to throw back his head and shout, *"Woe is me!"*

"Hey, Doc, what's wrong?" two or three of us asked at once.

"I'm ruined."

"How so?"

He turned his immense bulk to face us. "I've been moonlighting on the side, as a theatrical agent."

"No foolin'?"

"Yeah, and my most promising client, Dum Dum the Human Cannonball, just decided to retire."

Long-Drink looked puzzled. "Hey, what the hell, unemployment and everything, you shouldn't have any trouble lining up a replacement. Hell, if the money's right, *I'll* do it."

The Doc shook his head. "Dum-Dum is a midget. They cast the cannon special for him." He sipped bourbon and sighed. "I'm afraid we'll never see an artist of his caliber again."

Callahan howled, and the rest of us accorded the Doc the penultimate compliment: we held our noses and wept. He sat there in his special-built oversize chair and he looked grave, but you could see he was laughing, because he shook like jello. "Now I've got my own back for last night," he said. "Guess my riddles, will you?" He finished his bourbon. "Well, I'm off. Filling in tonight over at Smithtown General." His glass hit the exact center of the fireplace, and he strode out amid a thunderous silence.

We all crept back to our original seats and placed fresh orders. Callahan had barely finished medicating the wounded when the door banged open again. We turned, figuring that the Doc had thought of a topper, and were surprised.

Because young Tommy Janssen stood in the doorway, and tears were running down his face, and he was *stinking* drunk.

I got to him first. "Jesus, pal, what is it? Here, let me help you."

"Ricky's been kicking the gong—" he sang, quoting that old James Taylor song, "Junkie's Lament," and my blood ran cold. Could Tommy possibly have been stupid enough to . . . but no, that was booze on his breath, all right, and his sleeves were rolled up. I got him to a chair, and Callahan drew him a beer. He inhaled half of it, and cried some more. "Ricky," he sobbed. "Oh, Ricky, you stupid shit. He taught me how to smoke cigarettes, you know that?"

"Ricky who?"

"Ricky Maresca. We grew up together. We . . . we were junkies together once." He giggled though tears. "I turned him on, can you dig it? He turned me on to tobacco, I gave him his first taste of smack." His face broke. "Oh, *Christ!*"

"What's the matter with Ricky?" Callahan asked him.

"Nothing," he cried. "Nothing on Earth, baby. Ricky's got no problems at all."

"Jesus," I breathed.

"Oh, man. I *tried* to get him to come down here, do you know how hard I tried? I figured you guys could do it for him the way you did for me. Shit, I did everything but drag him here. I shoulda dragged him!" He broke down, and Josie hugged him.

After a while Callahan said, "Overdose?"

Tommy reached for his beer and knocked it spinning. "Shit, no. He tried to take off a gas station last night, for the monkey, and the pump jock had a piece in the desk. Ricky's down, man, he's down. All gone. Callahan, gimme a fucking whiskey!"

"Tommy," Callahan said gently, "let's talk awhile first,

have a little java, then we'll drink, OK?"

Tommy lurched to his feet and grabbed the bar for support. "Don't goddammit ever try to con a junkie! You think I've had enough, and you are seriously mistaken. Gimme a fuckin' whiskey or I'll come over there an' get it."

"Take it easy, son."

I tried to put my arm around Tommy.

"Hey, pal—"

He shoved me away. "Don't patronize me, Jake! *You* got wasted two nights running, why can't I?"

"I'll keep serving 'em as long as you can order 'em," Callahan said. "But son, you're close to the line now. Why don't you talk it out first? Whole idea of getting drunk is to talk it out before you pass out."

"Screw this," Tommy cried. "What the hell did I come here for, anyway? I can drink at home." He lurched in the general direction of the door.

"Tommy," I called, "wait up—"

"No," he roared. "Damn it, leave me alone, all of you! You hear me? I wanna be by myself, I—I'm not ready to talk about it yet. Just leave me the hell alone!" And he was gone, slamming the door behind him.

"Mike?" I asked.

"Hmmm." Callahan seemed of two minds. "Well, I guess you can't help a man who don't want to be helped. Let him go; he'll be in tomorrow." He mopped the bartop and looked troubled.

"You don't think he'll—"

"Go back to smack himself? I don't think so. Tommy hates that shit now. I'm just a little worried he might go look up Ricky's connection and try to kill him."

"Sounds like a good plan to me," Long-Drink muttered.

"But he's too drunk to function. More likely *he'll* go down. Or do a clumsy job and get busted for it."

"Be his second fall," I said.

"Damn it," the Drink burst out, "I'm goin' after him."

But when he was halfway to the door we all heard the sound of a vehicle door slamming out in the parking lot, and he pulled up short. "It's okay," he said. "That's my pickup, I'd know that noise anywhere. Tommy knows I keep a couple bottles under the seat in case of snakebite. He'll be okay—after a while I'll go find him and put him in the truckbed and take him home."

"Good man, Drink," I said. "Pyotr's out with the bug, we've got to cover for him."

Callahan nodded slowly. "Yeah, I guess that'll do it." The Place began to buzz again. I wanted a drink, and ordered more coffee instead, my seventh cup of the day so far. As it arrived, one of those accidental lulls in the conversation occurred, and we all plainly heard the sound of glass breaking out in the parking lot. Callahan winced, but spilled no coffee.

"How do you figure a thing like heroin, Mike? It seems to weed out the very stupid and the very talented. Bird, Lady Day, Tim Hardin, Janis, a dozen others we both know—and a half a million anonymous losers, dead in alleys and pay toilets and gas stations and other people's bedrooms. Once in every few thousand of 'em comes a Ray Charles or a James Taylor, able to put it down and keep on working."

"Tells you something about the world we're making. The very stupid and the very sensitive can't seem to live in it. Both kinds need dangerous doses of anesthetic just to get through a day. Be a lot less bother for all concerned if they could get it legal, I figure. If that Ricky wanted to die, okay—but he shouldn't have had to make some poor gas jockey have to shoot him."

Another sound of shattering glass from outside, as loud as the first.

"Hey Drink," Callahan said suddenly, "*how* much juice you say you keep in that truck?"

Long-Drink broke off a conversation with Margie Shorter. "Well, how I figure is, I got two hands—and besides, I might end up sharing the cab with somebody fastidious."

"Two *full* bottles?"

All of us got it at once, but the Drink was the first to move, and those long legs of his can really eat distance when they start swinging. He was out the door before the rest of us were in gear, and by the time we got outside he was just visible in the darkness, kneeling up on the tailgate of his pickup, shaking his head. Everybody started for the truck, but I waved them back and they heeded me. When I got to the truck there was just enough light to locate the two heaps of glass that had been full quarts of Jack Daniels once. The question was, how recently? I got down on my hands and knees, swept my fingers gingerly through the shards, accepting a few small cuts in exchange for the answer to the question, is the ground at all damp here abouts?

It was not.

"Jesus, Drink, he's sucked down two quarts of high test! Get him inside!"

"Can a man die from that?"

"Get him inside." Tommy has one of those funny stomachs, that won't puke even when it ought to; I was already running.

"Where are you—oh, right." I could hear him hauling Tommy off the truck. Callahan's phone was out of service that week, so the Drink knew where I had to be headed. He was only half right. I left the parking lot in a spray of gravel, slipped in dogshit just off the curb, nearly got creamed by a Friday-night cowboy in a Camaro, went up over the hood of a parked Caddy and burst in the door of the all-night deli across the street from Callahan's. The counterman spun around, startled.

"Bernie," I roared, "call the Doc at Smithtown. Alcohol overdose across the street, *stat,*" and then I was out the door again and sprinting up the dark street, heading for my second and most important destination.

Because I knew. Don't ask me how, I just knew. They say a hunch is an integration of data you did not know you possessed. Maybe I'd subconsciously begun to suspect just before the Doc had distracted me with his rotten pun—I'd had a lot of coffee, and they say coffee increases the I.Q. some. Maybe not—maybe I'd never have figured it out if

I hadn't *needed* to just then, if figuring it all out hadn't been the only thing that could save my silly-ass friend Tommy. I had no evidence that would stand up in any kind of court—only hints and guesswork. All I can tell you is that when I first cleared the doorway of Callahan's Place, I knew where I would end up going—hipping Bernie was only for back-up, and because it took so little time and was on the way.

Half a block is a short distance. Practically no distance at all. But to a man dreadfully hung over, afraid that his friend is dying, and above all absolutely, preternaturally *certain* of something that he cannot believe, a half block can take forever to run. By the time I got there, I believed. And then for the second time that day I was looking at a small, dark cottage with carven-Swiss drolleries around the windows and doors. This time I didn't care if I was welcome.

I didn't waste time on the door bell or the door. There was a big wooden lawn chair, maybe sixty or seventy pounds I learned later, but right then it felt like balsa as I heaved it up over my head and flung it through the big living room window. It took out the bulk of the window and the drapes behind; I followed it like Dum-Dum the Human Cannonball, at a slight angle, and God was kind: I landed on nothing but rug. I heard a distant shout in a language I did not know but was prepared to bet was Rumanian, and followed it through unfamiliar darkness, banging myself several times on hard objects, destroying an end table. Total dark, no moon or starlight, no time for matches, a door was before me and I kicked it open and there he was, just turning on a bedside lamp.

"I know," I said. "There's no more time for lying."

Pyotr tried to look uncomprehending, and failed, and there just wasn't any time for it.

"You don't drink blood. You *filter* it." He went white with shock. "I can even see how it must have happened, your trip at Callahan's, I mean. When you first got over here to the States, you must have landed in New York and got a job as a technician in a blood bank, right? Leach a *little* bit of nourishment out of a *lot* of whole blood you can feed without giving serious anemia to the transfusion patients. An ethical vampire—with a digestion that has trouble with beef broth. I'll bet you've even got big canines like the movie vampires—not because size makes them any more efficient at *letting* blood, but because there're some damned unusual glands in 'em. You interface with foreign blood and filter out the nourishment it carries in solution. Only you couldn't have known how they got blood in New York City, who the typical donor is, and before you knew it it was too late, you were a stone alcoholic." I was talking a mile a minute, but I could see every single shot strike home. I had no time to spare for his anguish; I grabbed him and hauled him off the bed, threw clothes at him. "Well, I don't give a shit about that now! You know young Tommy Janssen, well he's down the block with about three quarts of hooch in him, and the last two went down in a gulp apiece, so you move your skinny Transylvanian ass or I'll kick it off your spine, you got me? *Jump,* goddammit!"

He caught on at once, and without a word he pulled his clothes on, fast enough to suit me. An instant later we were sprinting out the door together.

The half-block run gave me enough time to work out how I could do this without blowing Pyotr's cover. It was the total blackness of the night that gave me the idea. When we reached Callahan's I kept on running around to the back, yelling at him to follow. As we burst in the door to the back room I located the main breaker and killed it, yanking a few fuses for insurance. The lights went out and the icebox stopped sighing. Fortunately I don't need light to find my way around Callahan's Place, and good night-sight must have been a favorable adaptation for anyone with Pyotr's basic mutation; we were out in the main room in seconds and in silence.

At least compared with the hubbub there; everybody was shouting at once. I cannoned into Callahan in the darkness—

I saw the glowing cheroot-tip go past my cheek—and I hugged him close and said in his ear, "Mike, trust me. Do *not* find the candles you've got behind the bar. And open the windows."

"Okay, Jake," he said calmly at once, and moved away in the blackness. With the windows open, matches blew out as fast as they could be lit. The shouting intensified. In the glow of one attempted match-lighting, I saw Tommy laid out on the bar in the same place Lady Macbeth had lain the night before, and I saw Pyotr reach him. I sprang across the room to the fireplace—thank God it was a warm night; no fire—and cupped my hands around my mouth.

"ALL RIGHT, PEOPLE," I roared as loud as I could, and silence fell.

Damned if I can remember what I said. I guess I told them that the Doc was on the way, and made up some story about the power failure, and told a few lies about guys I'd known who drank twice as much booze and survived, and stuff like that. All I know is that I *held* them, by sheer force of vocal personality, kept their attention focused on me there in the dark for perhaps four or five minutes of impassioned monologue. While behind them, Pyotr worked at the bar.

When I heard him clear his throat I began winding it down. I heard the distant sound of a door closing, the door that leads from the back room to the world outside. "So the important thing," I finished, locating one of those artificial logs in the dark and laying it on the hearth, "is not to panic and to wait for the ambulance," and I lit the giant crayon and stacked real maple and birch on top of it. The fire got going at once, and that sorted out most of the confusion. Callahan was bending over Tommy, rubbing at the base of his neck with a bar-rag, and he looked up and nodded. "I think he's okay, Jake. His breathing is a lot better."

A ragged cheer went up.

By the time we had the lights back on, the wagon arrived, Doc Webster bursting in the door like a crazed hippo with three attendants following him. I stuck around just long enough to hear him confirm that Tommy would pull through, promised Callahan I'd give him the yarn later, and slipped out the back.

Walking the half block was much more enjoyable than running it. I found Pyotr in his bedroom. Roaring drunk, of course, reeling around the room and swearing in Rumanian.

"Hi, Pyotr. Sorry I bust your window."

"Sodomize the window. Jake, is he—"

"Fine. You saved his life."

He frowned ferociously and sat down on the floor. "It is no good, Jake. I thank you for trying to keep my secret, but it will not work."

"No, it won't."

"I cannot continue. My conscience forbids. I have helped young Janssen. But it must end. I am ripping you all up."

"Off, Pyotr. Ripping us off. But don't kick yourself too hard. What choice did you have? And you saved a lot of the boys a lot of hangovers, laundering their blood the way you did. Just happens I've got a trick metabolism, so instead of skimming off my hangover, you gave me one. And doubled your own: the blood I gave you the last two nights must have been no prize."

"I stole it."

"Well, maybe. You didn't rob me of the booze—we *both* got drunk on it. You *did* rob me of a little nourishment—but I gather you also 'robbed' me of a considerable amount of poisonous byproducts of fatigue, poor diet, and prolonged despair. So maybe we come out even."

He winced and rolled his eyes. "These glands in my teeth—that was a very perceptive guess, Jake—are unfortunately not very selective. Alcoholism was not the only unpleasant thing I picked up working at the blood bank—another splendid guess—although it is the only one that has persisted. But it must end. Tomorrow night when I am capable I will go to Mr. Callahan's Place and confess what

I have been doing—and then I will move somewhere else
to dry out, somewhere where they do not buy blood from
winos. Perhaps back to the Old Country." He began to sob
softly. "In many ways it will be a relief. It has been *hard,*
has made me ashamed to see all of you thinking I was some
kind of *altruist,* when all the time I was—" He wept.

"Pyotr, listen to me." I sat on the floor with him. "Do
you know what the folks are going to do tomorrow night
when you tell them?"

Headshake.

"Well, *I* do, sure as God made little green thingies to
seal plastic bags with, and so do you if you think about it.
I'm so certain, I'm prepared to bet you a hundred bucks in
gold right now."

Puzzled stare; leaking tears.

"They'll take up a collection for you, asshole!"

Gape.

"You've been hanging out there for years, now, you *know*
I'm right. Every eligible man and woman there is a blood
donor already, the Doc sees to that—do you mean to tell
me they'd begrudge another half liter or so for a man who'd
leave a warm bed in the middle of the night to risk his cover
and save a boy's life?"

He began to giggle drunkenly. "You know—hee, hee—
I believe you are right." The giggle showed his fangs. Suddenly it vanished. "Oh," he cried, "I do not deserve such
friends. Do you know what first attracted me about Callahan's Place? There is no mirror. No, no, not that silly su-
perstition—mirrors reflect people like me as well as anyone.
That's just it. *I was ashamed to look at my reflection in a
mirror."*

I made him look at me. "Pyotr, listen to me. You worked
hard for your cakes and ale, these last few years. You kept
a lot of silly bastards from turning into highway statistics.
Okay, you may have had *another* motive that we didn't
know—but underneath it all, you're just like everybody
else at Callahan's Place."

"Eh?"

"A sucker for your friends."

And it broke him up, thank God, and everything worked out just fine.

And a couple of weeks later, Pyotr played us all a couple of fabulous Rumanian folk songs—on Lady Macbeth.

AUTHOR'S NOTE

I should have known better.

When, in the first appearance of "Pyotr's Story" (*Analog* Oct. 12, 1981), I left six riddles unsolved, and published my address at the end of the story, offering a chit good for a free drink at Callahan's to any reader who correctly deduced the answer and the category—well, let's face it, I did anticipate that I might notice a slight bulge in my mail for a while. I mean, I *was* asking for it, there's no argument there.

Be careful what you ask for; you might receive it.

I used to publish my mailing address regularly in book-review columns for *Galaxy* magazine, and each appearance was good for from five to twenty letters a week over the ensuing month. I knew that *Analog* had a significantly larger readership than *Galaxy,* and adjusted my expectations accordingly—I thought. I projected perhaps a hundred responses, a hundred and fifty tops.

I did not keep a fully accurate accounting, but I would estimate that as of February 9, 1982 I had received somewhere between 800 and 1,000 pieces of mail as a result of that fool riddle contest.

As soon as the first sack arrived (that's not hyperbole: I mean a full sack of mail, the first of several), I took in the situation, grasped the full extent of my folly (don't let on; grasping your folly in public is illegal in Nova Scotia), and, with the cool aplomb and courage-under-fire which has made my name a sellword on Wall Street, instantly formed a dynamic plan: I kicked the sack into a corner and fled the country. My wife Jeanne (founder and Artistic Director of **Nova Dance Theatre**, the finest Modern dance company in Canada) had received a providential invitation to perform with Beverly Brown Dancensemble: Theatre for Bodies And Voices, at the Riverside Dance Festival in what David Letterman refers to as "one of the more interesting cities in the tri-state area," New York—so I threw my suitcase, my typewriter, my child and my Ray Charles tapes into the trunk of the car and went with her. And sacks of mail grew in her dance studio behind us in Halifax (for it was that address I put in *Analog*, in a feeble attempt to divert process-servers)...

And then some helpful soul at DancExchange forwarded all those sacks to us in New York.

Since I had expected to be answering those letters from Canada, where U.S. stamps are worthless, I had carefully requested that respondents enclose an International Reply Coupon (supposed, by law, to be obtainable at any post office in the U.S. or Canada). Some 25 percent of respondents failed to follow this injunction, enclosed U.S. stamps or nothing at all, but forget that a moment: here I am on Manhattan Island in August with about 400 to 500 IRCs in my hands, and I wait in line for an hour and a quarter in the post office (a structure to which the Black Hole of Calcutta is frequently favorably compared for summertime comfort), and when finally I stagger up to the window, a surly homunculus with a genuinely incredible goiter informs me, with immense satisfaction, that regulations forbid him to accept more than 10 IRCs at a time. I whip out my calculator: 500 IRCs at 10 per transaction at 1.25 hours per transaction = 62.5 hours on line, or roughly eight days...

So I burned petrol and wasted cargo space to haul those sacks back home to Halifax. Where I united them with their less-traveled cousins, which had arrived in our absence, and settled down to answering the goddammed things...

Tabulations:

Oddly, the ratio of right to wrong answers remained rock-constant: every time I stopped and ran subtotals, it ran almost precisely two right answers for every wrong. Call it a 67 percent success rate for the *Analog* audience as a group. (Some of the wrong answers were absolutely brilliant!)

The only correlation I noted of any significance was that responses which came on university departmental letterhead were usually wrong—and several of the exceptions turned out to be grad students or TAs using their professor's stationery. In other words, holders of tenure at institutes of higher education averaged dumber than the general populace or any other discernible group in the sample.

Another thing I found instructive about all this was the performance of *Analog* readers (certainly not an undereducated group) in following the simplest of explicit written instructions. I had asked that each respondent enclose a self-addressed envelope or SAE along with the above-mentioned IRC. Now, some few readers claimed ignorance of IRCs, or said that their local postmaster claimed ignorance, and the expedients they tried instead were many and various. Three or four sent *cash*, and of those only one was bright enough to send *Canadian* cash. (In those palmy days of yesteryear, the Canadian/American exchange rate hovered around par, which meant I took a conversion-fee bath on the money.) But at least 10 percent of the responses I received contained *no* return postage—and the rate-to-States *doubled* the month I got home to Halifax. (The royalty I will eventually receive for this particular book you hold in your hands comes to less than the present cost of a Canadian stamp—considerably less if you live in the States. And they're talking about raising the rates again.) Postageless letters that were not particularly amusing or endearing were used to insulate the attic. And 25 percent of respondents enclosed no return-address envelope: same doctrine applied.

It wasn't a total loss, even when you figure in the cost of Xeroxing form letters (one for right answers, one for wrong) and the postage and envelopes I got burned for, and the hours of work-time lost, and the wear and tear on my tongue (did you ever lick a thousand envelopes and several hundred stamps?). For one thing, I took the opportunity to make up a *third* form letter—a press release listing all the books I had in print and where to get them and such—and folded one into every envelope. For another, I was able to insulate my entire attic and make a start on the root cellar.

For another, the vast majority of the letters I got were *delightful!*

Some were hilarious. Some were heart-warming. Some were ingenious. Some were touching. Some were enlightening. Remarkably few "faded into the woodwork," became just one-more-goddam-letter-to-be-processed—in any event, I didn't get any complaints from Mike Callahan regarding the people who came to cash in their chits. (Of course, I just provided the chit—*finding* the Place was their problem.) Taken all together, the response pleased me, cheered and encouraged me in my work.

On the other hand, a substantial number of respondents enclosed riddles of their own—enough to make a life-size fully detailed papier maché replica of the Space Shuttle. I'm sure they were all disappointed that I didn't try to answer their no-doubt ingenious riddles, but honest to God, there are thousands!

And that's not the worst. The worst is that *the damned responses are still coming in to this day!*

Analog is published all around the planet, with a translation lag that apparently ranges up to a couple of years. Furthermore, people keep coming across back issues in libraries and second-hand bookstores, stumbling over the riddle-contest, and uttering small cries of delight.

I arbitrarily established a cut-off date, and stopped sending chits some time in mid-1982. (For one thing, my tab at Callahan's started reaching the proportions of the American

National Debt.) I have kept to that—indeed, as you will
shortly learn, it is no longer possible for me to supply any
chits—but I still feel a faint twinge of guilt every time I
get another letter that begins, "Dear Mr. Robinson, I think
I've solved Doc Webster's riddles—"

And the last thing I want is to compound the problem
here.

So no, I'm not going to publish my mailing address here,
and no, I will not issue any more drink-chits, and yes, I am
going to put the answers to the unsolved riddles below. If
you want to solve them for yourself first, skip them. If you
solve them successfully, don't tell me about it. And no,
frankly, I'm not overwhelmingly interested in trying to de-
cipher your riddles, however clever and funny they may be.
In the immortal words of disc jockey Don Imus, "Keep
those cards and letters!"

No, that's not true. I love getting mail, and I need audience feedback to continue growing in my work. By all
means drop me a line in care of Berkley Books—especially
if you can find it in your head to enclose SAE and IRC.

Just don't mention riddles.

Or use the word "trilogy."

The Answers to Doc Webster's Riddles:

The category is "Male American Politicians," or any variant
thereof. The individual answers are:

   a) irrigated; laser pistol = runneled; ray gun =
   Ronald Reagan

   b) Nazi; cook lightly = Jerry; brown = *Jerry
   Brown*

   c) British punk; knowledge, current = Teddy;
   ken, eddy = *Teddy Kennedy*

d) chicken coop; foreplay = hennery; kissing her = *Henry Kissinger*

e) wealthier; nuts to = richer; nix on = *Richard Nixon*

An embarassing thing happened. Astute readers will have noted that I also left riddle IIe) unsolved. When the responses started coming in, I discovered that this riddle had proved the hardest: everybody wanted to know who "coffin; baby boy" was. The problem was that I had, by this point, mislaid my first draft of "Pyotr's Story"—and I had forgotten the solution. To my horror, I found that I could not figure it out myself!

After months of shame, I sat bolt upright in bed one morning and realized I had the solution again—so I incorporated it into the story you are about to read, "Involuntary Man's Laughter."

One last word about "Pyotr's Story," though. If by any chance you missed its several respectful salutes to William Goldman, I hope you will seize the next opportunity to run out and purchase his immortal classic, *The Princess Bride*.

CHAPTER 3

Involuntary Man's Laughter

SOME OF THE people who hang out at Callahan's Place aren't all there — this is widely known. But a few of them aren't there at all.

Well, obviously they *are* there, at least in a sense. Otherwise I'd be offering you a paradox, and Sam Webster is the only Doc we have here at Callahan's bar. But if a customer cannot be seen, heard, felt, smelt, or dealt a hand of cards, if he casts no shadow, empties no glass, and never visits the men's room — can he really be said to be there? Even if you're having a conversation with him at the time?

We have two or three regulars at Callahan's who fit that nondescription: old and dear friends of ours who have never set foot in the place. One of them, for instance, is a ghost, and I'll tell you about him another time, when we've both had a couple more drinks. But the one I'd like to tell you about right now is a human being — and while I have seen him once, I don't think I ever will again.

It was a Punday Night last year when the Cheerful Charlies showed up looking glum. This was quite unusual, enough so to engage my attention when I caught sight of them both — for the Cheerful Charlies have, quite literally, earned their name.

Doc Webster had already won the Punday competition — something he does with about the same consistency with which Mr. T wins arguments. The only way the Doc can possibly lose is if all possible puns on a given topic have been exhausted before it's his turn — and far more often, when everyone else has come up empty, the Doc still has four or five up his sleeve. You might say that our chronic asteismus is iatrogenic . . . but of course you probably wouldn't.

Like now, for instance: the evening's topic had been one of those so broad as to seem inexhaustible—"animals"— and owl give ewe the gnus: most of us cats and chicks were falcon hoarse as we toad the lion and shrew our glasses into the fire in sheepish cabitchulation. But Dog Websteer was still game, cheerfoal as venison the springtime, a weaselly grin on his puss that got my goat.

"—always puzzled me," he was saying, "that females of all species except the human seem, at best, utterly disinterested in mating. Most will actively resist it until compelled by glandular pressure, and even then seem to derive little enjoyment from the business. Why, I wondered, should human females alone be blessed with the capacity to enjoy the inevitable?"

A good question. I'd always wondered that myself.

"The answer turns out to be simple. Man is a *bald* ape."

"Oh, God," Shorty Steinitz groaned. "Even for you, Doc, that's an *awful* pun."

The Doc blinked and then grinned. "You misunderstand me, sir—for once the pun was unintentional. No, I mean that man is relatively hairless—whereas, through some sadistic quirk of nature, most other male animals are endowed with hairy penises. A cat's penis, for instance, is covered with short, spiky hairs—*which face in the wrong direction*."

Murmurs of surprise and sympathy ran around the tavern; a few ladies winced.

"Small wonder, then," the Doc went on, folding his hands across his expansive belly, "that a female cat doesn't much feel like putting out—for any tom dickin' hairy."

The horrified silence stretched out for nearly five seconds . . . and then we awarded him the Supreme Accolade: as one we left our drinks where they stood, held our noses, and fled screaming into the night.

It was a nice night out there (not that that matters to any

friend of Mickey Finn these days); I found that I was in no hurry to follow the rest of the gang back inside. My drink was perfectly safe where it was, and I wanted a few minutes alone with myself. I was feeling ... well, "troubled" would be too strong a word, but I don't know a word for the shading between there and "content." Just one of those mild itches of the soul that a man doesn't particularly feel like sharing with all his friends, a passing impulse to toot for a few bars on the old self-pity horn.

It was, perhaps inevitably, just as I was finishing a contemplative cigarette and saying "Sometime again," to the full moon that the Cheerful Charlies drove up in their '54 Thunderbird and wedged it into the confusion. (By honored custom, the parking lot at Callahan's always looks as though a platoon of psychopaths had turned a game of Bumper Cars into an unresolvable snarl and wandered off. A half-dozen times a night we all have to pile outside to let somebody out, and it doesn't inconvenience us in the least.) Just the sight of their splendid old heap cheered me up some.

Neither of them is named Charlie; that's their professional designation and job description. They cheer people up for a living. You may have seen their ad in the paper:

DEPRESSED? Gamble a little time on The Cheerful Charlies. $25 if we cheer you up, nothing at all if we don't: you decide! 24-hr. emergency service available (rates double from 10 P.M. to 8 A.M. Call CHE-ERUP for an appointment: What have you got to lose?

And, of course, their business card sums it up even more succinctly: HAVE FUN, WILL TRAVEL.

They did not found the business. That was done by Tom Flannery a few years back. Tom was one of the most infectiously cheerful men I ever met, and he had a certain natural advantage in cheering people up: at the time he founded his enterprise, Tom had about eight months to go on the nine-month sentence his doctors had given him (and did in fact eventually die on schedule almost to the day).

He didn't talk about it much, but it made a terrific hole-card for dealing with cases of intractable self-pity. How many people have the gall to be depressed around a smiling fellow who says he'll be dead before your tax-return comes back? Tom hadn't expected to make money at his job—but to his surprise he left a sizable estate.

The present Cheerful Charlies began as clients of Tom's. Each was depressed by the same two things: both were chronically unemployed, and both bore names of the sort that parents ought to be prevented by law or by vigilante violence from giving to their children. The Moore family pronounced their name "More," and saw fit to name their son Les; while the Gluehams, with a malignant case of the cutes, named their daughter Merry.

The coincidence of names was just too much for Tom Flannery to resist, I guess. He convinced them both that one of the best ways to cheer yourself up is to try and cheer other people up (it worked for him, after all), and took them both on as apprentices, thus solving their un-employment problem. As he must have hoped, they fell in love—and when they married, they solved the question of does-she-take-his-last-name by swapping even-steven. With irresistible appropriateness, she became Merry Moore and he became Les Glueham. They carried on Tom's business after he died, and the story of their names itself is sometimes sufficient to get a client smiling.

Les and Merry have no set routine, but rather a whole spectrum of techniques which they tailor to fit the individual case. They are wise and warm people, with professionally tuned empathic faculties, and they seem to have made a remarkably comfortable marriage. One of their early cases, for instance, was a lonely old widower who had lost all his joy in living: after all their best efforts had failed, Merry and Les talked it over, decided that it might help and that in this specific case it probably couldn't hurt—and then Merry took the old gentleman to bed. It did the trick, and since then they have (very infrequently) had occasions to use lovemaking as cheer-up therapy, singly or together. It has always worked so far, and they always refuse their fee in such cases. This is both to avoid breaking laws, and to motivate themselves to exhaust all other possibilities before resorting to Old Reliable-But-Risky; it inhibits the human tendency to rationalize oneself into the sack. But some cases of depression will yield to no other medicine.

And if even *that* doesn't work, Merry and Les bring 'em to Callahan's Place.

But they didn't appear to have a client with them tonight. They got out of the T-Bird, a little slowly I thought, and came my way. Merry was carrying something that looked like a big piece of stereo gear, and Les seemed to have a hardcover book with him. "Hey, Jake—what's the matter?" Merry called to me.

"God's teeth," I said under my breath. Then aloud: "From twenty feet across a parking lot by moonlight you can tell I've got something on my mind. From what? The echo of an expression I was wearing before you pulled up? You people are incorrigibly good at what you do, you know that?"

"Ouch," Les said softly.

They had almost reached me by now, and the third thing I saw was that Les's hardcover was a boxed videotape, and the second thing I saw was that Merry's stereo was a VCR, and the first thing I saw was that Les and Merry were— astonishingly, most uncharacteristically—miserably depressed. Their expressions, their stride, their body language, all said that they were so far down that up was for astronomers; they had, to quote a song of mine, the Industrial Strength Blues.

"Jesus Christ on a Moped, what's the matter with you two?" An unpleasant thought began to form. "Oh hell, you didn't lose one, did you?" That happened a year ago, a sleeping-pill job, and it took us all about a week to put the Cheerful Charlies back together again. It is the occupational risk, and a failure rate as low as one a year means that the Cheerfuls are supernaturally good at what they do.

(They have to be; there is no malpractice insurance for their racket.)

"No," Merry answered, "not yet anyway."

"Well, *tell* me about it."

"You tell us yours first."

"Mine? Hey, on a scale of ten I'm a point two five and you guys are up in the eights—and I think it's a log scale, like the Richter."

"Come on, give. If it's a simple one, great: we could use the confidence right now."

I shrugged. "Okay. I was just going a few rounds with envy."

"Of whom?" Merry asked, setting the VCR down on the Datsun I was using for a bench.

"The Doc."

"Ah."

"I like to make people laugh. So I troll for the best jokes I can find, make up the best ones I can devise, work on my timing, try to work the audience into it and use their feedback—and it works pretty well, most times they laugh, or groan, or whatever I was looking for. The Doc could recite his Social Security Number, deadpan, and lay 'em on the floor. Dammit, I tell better jokes than he does, I even think I tell 'em better—and he gets more laughs. With his incredibly tortuous set-ups and his corny voice and his Paleozoic punchlines, we all fall down laughing. Even me! He's just an intrinsically funny man—and I'm just a guy who tries to be funny."

"And the worst of it," Les said, "is that he's such a totally nice guy, you can't even dislike him for it."

"Bullseye."

Merry grinned, a ghost of her usual grin. "This is ironic." She and Les shared a glance.

I shook my head ruefully. "For you guys, no doubt. So okay: in the words of Mr. Ribadhee to the Hip Ghand, 'Straighten me, 'cause I'm ready.'"

"Jake," Les said, "a few years ago you lent us a novel called *Lord of Light,* by Roger Zelazny. Remember it?"

"Sure. An SF novel about a world patterned after Hindu mythology."

"Right—and then along came Buddha to kick over the applecart. Now, remember how the people who had become 'gods' were each able, at will, to take on an Aspect and raise up an Attribute?"

"Yama could become Death, and drink your life with his eyes, Mara's Aspect was Illusion, and his Attribute was to cloud your mind with a gesture. And so forth."

"You've got it. Well, it's like that with the Doc. His Aspect is Humor. In a figurative, but very real sense, Doc Webster *is* Humor—at least when he chooses to take on his Aspect. And his Attribute is the ability to make you piss yourself laughing. Envying him is like envying a flower because it never needs deodorant."

"Huh," I said. "I think I get you. It's silly to envy the gods."

"Especially when you are one."

"*Eh?*"

"Jake," Merry said, "when was the last time someone interrupted you while you were singing?"

"Well..." I couldn't bring such an instance to mind. People do tend to quiet down when I take my guitar out of her case.

Les did his uncanny Martin Mull imitation. "'Remember the Great Folk Music Scare of the Fifties?'" he quoted. "'That shit almost caught on.' Jake, haven't you noticed that you're about the only folksinger left on Long Island who can still find regular work? Don't you know why you don't need electronics and a thousand watts and a rhythm section to get gigs? Man, when you pick up Lady Macbeth and put her across your lap and open your mouth, you take on your Aspect—and when you wring her neck and coax sound out of her sounding-box and sing along with her, you're raising up your Attribute. You take people out of themselves, for as long as you choose to go on singing. Doc Webster is Humor, Jake, and you are Music. Don't you know that?"

I thought it over—and suddenly grinned. "How did you guys ever get the name Cheerful Charlies?"

"Maybe because we own the complete works of Walt Kelly," Les hazarded. "Come on, let's go inside."

"Wait—what about *your* problem? Cheering-up ought to be like breastfeeding, you know, mutually satisfactory."

"Tit for tot?" Merry asked innocently.

Les mock-glared at her. "I think our problem should be taken inside," he said. "We need a group head on this one."

So we went in and took chairs at the bar.

Mike Callahan came ambling over, wiping his big hands on his apron, smiling broadly when he saw the Cheerfuls. He took out one of the *non*-safety stick matches he imports from Canada, struck it on his stubbly chin, and put a fresh light on one of the stunted malodorous cigars he imports from Hell. "Well, if it ain't the Beerful Barleys! What'll it be, folks?"

I finished the beer I had left on the counter and answered for all three of us. "Bless us father, for we have thirst."

Callahan nodded and made up three portions of God's Blessing. It is called Irish Coffee by the vulgar, and I'm told there are actually places where they don't sugar the rim of the glass before making it—but we who drink at Callahan's Place have a proper respect for the finer things in life. "Here you go, folks." I could tell from his expression that Mike had picked up on the Cheerfuls' state of mind, and wanted to know what they were down about. But . . . look, I've been hanging out at Callahan's for a good many years now. But if I walked in tomorrow night with a toilet bowl tattooed on my forehead, Mike Callahan would fail to notice it unless and until I brought the matter up. Mike likes that people should open up and talk about their troubles in his bar—and so he has given standing orders to Fast Eddie the piano player that anyone caught asking snoopy questions is to be discouraged with a blackjack.

Occasionally, though, he will allow himself to lead a witness. "So how's life been treating you?" he asked as he Blessed us.

Merry answered obliquely. "Mike, is that babble box in the back room still operational?"

The big Irishman blinked. "Well, yeah. I use it for a monitor on my microprocessor."

Callahan's Place has been fully wired for cable television—but the only times in my memory that the tube has ever been hooked up for viewing and switched on were coronations, assassinations, space shots, and the final episode of "M*A*S*H." Its operation requires either the unanimous vote of all customers present, or—even more rarely—whim of Mike Callahan.

Merry lifted the VCR from her lap and set it on the bar. "Would you whip it out, Mike? We want to call a meeting."

The red-headed barkeep was as mystified and curious as I was—I could tell—but he just nodded.

Well, of course, by the time the boob tube was hot and the VCR connected, the Cheerfuls had the undivided attention of everyone in the room. Callahan passed around fresh drinks for those who needed them, and we sat back to see what the Cheerfuls had for us.

"Folks," Merry said, popping the tape into the deck and laying her finger on the PLAY button, "we've got a client we don't know what to do with, and we'd like to ask your help."

There was a ragged chorus of reply. "Sure," "Of course," "You got it," and, from Long-Drink McGonnigle in the corner, "Whyn't you just bring him or her around?"

Merry looked pained. "Ordinarily we would. But this case is a little unique, and we thought it might be advisable if we prepared you first. You may not be able to help us, and if you can't it'll hurt worse than not trying."

"I am offended," the Drink said, only half-kidding. "This here is *Callahan's Place*. Did you need to prepare us before you brought around that guy with no jaw?"

"No," Merry conceded, "and you were all splendid. But this is different."

"We just have to be sure," Les said. "This guy is right on the edge. So here's the deal: the tape Merry is about to run lasts about two minutes. If you can all watch it all the

way through in dead silence—without a single sound—
we'll bring him around tomorrow night. Deal?"

"This tape is of your client?" Callahan asked.

"That's right."

"Piece of cake," Long-Drink stated. "Fire it up."

Merry nodded, and pushed down the PLAY button—
—and we all fell down laughing.

She stopped the tape, and the laughter chopped off rag-
gedly, leaving a stunned silence.

She reached to start it again, and we redoubled our de-
termination not to laugh . . . and within five seconds the last
of us had collapsed again in helpless, horrified laughter.

She stopped and started it once more, and this time I bit
my tongue hard enough to draw blood, and again I could
not prevent myself from whooping with laughter. Nor could
any of us—Callahan included.

"You see why your problem outside seemed so ironic to
us, Jake," Merry murmured, stopping the tape for the last
time and popping it up out of the machine. I nodded, thunderstruck.

Did you ever find yourself in a situation where it is
hideously inappropriate to laugh—and you just can't help
yourself? It is a horrid sensation, much like shitting your
pants. Now I began to understand why the Cheerfuls weren't.
Imagine if Doc Webster literally *couldn't* help being funny . . .

"What de fuck was dat?" Fast Eddie breathed.

"That," Doc Webster said grimly, "was the worst case
of Tourette's Syndrome I ever saw in my life."

"Doc," Long-Drink said indignantly, "are you trying to
tell me that that was some kind of *disease?* What kind of
guy do you think God is, anyway?"

So the Doc told us all about Tourette's Syndrome. Nobody knows what causes it. You may have seen Dick Cavett
doing a public-service commercial about it, late at night
when the network has run out of paying customers. I had—
and recognized the symptoms almost as quickly as the Doc
had—but it was hard to imagine that there could be an

unhappier victim anywhere in the world than the Cheerfuls' client; he was afflicted with an extremely exaggerated version of the syndrome.

The symptoms of Tourette's include involuntary twitching, grunting and barking. No sufferer is happy with it—but this young fellow just happened to have a recurring twitch that looked *exactly* like what might be produced by the greatest comedian in the world going flat out for a laugh, and his grunts sounded *precisely* like a gorilla making love, and his constant barking was not only *uncannily* canine, but issued from a face which looked more like a cocker spaniel's than even early-period Ringo Starr did. The overall effect was devastatingly—diabolically—hilarious; the three symptoms, funny enough separately, heterodyned together.

"His name is Billy Walker, and he's eighteen years old," Les said. "The disease came on at age fifteen—it usually hits the young—and the usual palliatives, Haldol and so forth, don't help him in the slightest. Unlike most sufferers, he can't suppress or control his symptoms, even for a short time. This tape was made by a couple of specialists from Johns Hopkins, and they had to leave the room while the camera was rolling or they would have spoiled the audio track. For the last two years Billy has lived shut up in a little cottage in Rocky Point, supported by his parents. The only friend he's had since the onset was a blind and deaf guy he met at Hopkins. They lived together for a year. The guy died two weeks ago, and Billy saw our ad and got in touch with us."

"And now I don't know what we're going to do for him," Merry finished sadly.

"How'd he get in touch with you?" I asked.

Merry looked even sadder. "I hate to admit this. He called us three times on the phone, and each time we just assumed that it was a gag call. The third time, Les got mad and told him off—so he sent us a letter."

"How could he hold a pen steady enough with a twitch like that?"

"He couldn't. He typed the letter, timing the twitches."

"Jesus."

"As if things weren't bad enough, of course, he happens to be extremely intelligent and sensitive, with the remnants of what was once a terrific sense of humor."

"You've spent time with him?" Callahan asked.

"With great difficulty, about half an hour," Merry said. "The longest I could go without giggling was about ten or twenty seconds, and eventually I gave up, assured him that I had something terrific up my sleeve, and got out of there. My ribs still hurt. There's something about that bark that you just can't get used to. Look, does *anyone* here have any idea what we could do for this poor son of a bitch? He's so damned *lonely* that the tears pour down your face while you're laughing, honest to God."

There was a general rumble of sad negation. "Beats the hell out of me." "Help the poor guy do himself in as painlessly as possible." "Maybe it'll go away . . . in time." "Find a whole lot of blind and deaf guys . . . nah, that's no good." Les and Merry looked more and more downcast.

"I think I got it," Callahan said, and they both looked around sharply, hope beginning to form. "Hey, Drink! Lend me your copper-topper a minute, will you?"

The McGonnigle, puzzled but willing, tossed Mike the night-watchman's cap that he wears off-duty (because it looks so much like a policeman's hat that he is never ever passed, cut off, or tailgated on the highway). Mike caught it, opened the cash register and took out a fistful of bills, dropped them into the hat.

"Ladies and gentlemen," he boomed, "I'm looking for about three hundred bucks." And he passed the hat to me.

I looked around, saw there were about fifty or sixty of us present, and tossed in a fin. Then I remembered how many of the regulars had lost jobs lately, and added another five, and passed the hat on.

When it got back to Callahan it was overflowing with cash. He totaled it up, and it came to four and a quarter. He beamed around at us all. "Thanks, folks. The cash register just closed for the night." And he began a bucket-brigade of fresh drinks for everyone present.

"Whaddya gonna do wit de cabbage, Boss?" Fast Eddie asked.

"You'll see tomorrow night, Eddie. Or maybe the night after; it might take a while to set up."

"Set up *what?*" Les and Merry chorused.

"Meet me here tomorrow at noon and I'll show you," Callahan promised.

The next evening was Fireside Fill-More Night, on which Fast Eddie and I traditionally jam together. There were four people missing that I had expected to see: the Cheerfuls, Eddie and Callahan himself. Tom Hauptmann, the second-string bartender, could tell us nothing except that Mike had called him late in the day and asked him to fill in. So I did a solo, and it went well enough . . . but halfway through I got an idea, and invited Doc Webster up to do a bunch of comedy songs—and we brought the house down together.

I pulled in the next night at about a quarter to eight. Callahan was there in his usual place behind the bar, and Tom Hauptmann was with him. That was a little odd: Mike usually only needs help on weekends, when the crowd is thickest, and there weren't enough customers tonight to justify two barkeeps. The TV (no, not Bill Gerrity; I mean the television) was back on the bartop, but the station it was tuned to didn't seem to be on the air; horizontal stripes chased each other up its face. Callahan saw me come in, sized me up with a glance and had a shot of Bushmill's and a beer ready by the time I reached him. As usual, it was just what I'd have ordered if he'd given me a chance. "Evening, Jake."

"Hi, Mike. How'd you make out on that Billy Walker thing?"

He drew on his cheroot. "We'll find out together at nine o'clock."

"Okay, be mysterious." I sipped and chased a few times, enjoying the contrast of tastes and textures. "Hey, where's the blackboard? This *is* Riddle Night, isn't it?"

On Riddle Night, one of us makes up riddles and the rest of us try and unscramble them. Each solved riddle costs the Riddlemaster/Riddlemistress a drink; each unresolved riddle is a free drink for him/her. Most often we use the classic "Invisible Idiot" or mangled-translation format. You must have heard the old dodge about the translator who rendered "out of sight, out of mind" literally as "invisible idiot." Like that. For example, "festive, meathooks; finish second" would be correctly deciphered as "gala, hands; place" or "Callahan's Place." Semicolons mark the end of a word, commas separate parts of a single word. They can get quite tricky—it once took me months to translate "coffin; baby boy" as Paul Newman. Ordinarily the Riddlemaster (last week's champ) would have had at least half a dozen riddles already chalked up on a big blackboard by the door for study—but last week's champ was Callahan himself, and he hadn't even trotted out the board yet. "We'll get to them later, too," he said, and wandered off to replenish the free lunch.

So I washed down my curiosity with the world's oldest whiskey (they got their charter to distill in 1608) and listened to Fast Eddie stitch his way through a medley of Eubie Blake, Willie the Lion, Pinetop Smith, and Memphis Slim. Eddie had to get special hammers for his piano; the thumbtacks used to keep falling out. I was mildly sorry I'd left my guitar at home; I'd missed my weekly jam with him. The joint filled up while he played, and our spirits danced to his merry tune. When Eddie's on a roll like that, people tend to shut up and dig it. Once a loud newcomer distracted the runty little piano man in the middle of "Tricky Fingers." Eddie got the sap from his boot and pegged it across the room, laid the fellow out, and damned if the sap didn't bounce back right to his hand—and not a note did he fluff during the procedure. They raise 'em tough in Red Hook.

About the time my hands were getting sore from clapping time with him, Eddie went into a classic bar-room walkout and nailed it shut behind him, to thunderous applause. A storm of empty glasses converged on the fireplace and shattered together in tribute, and the two bartenders were busy for a time. And then Callahan called for order. I glanced at my watch; it was nearly nine.

"Ladies and gentlemen and regular customers," he announced, "tonight is Riddle Night. By our customs, I am Riddlemaster, on account of I wiped the floor with you mugs last week. But I'm yielding the floor—or at least part of the counter—to a guest Riddlemaster." He reached under the bar, and took out a flat object patchcorded to the back of the television. His microprocessor keyboard. He did something to it, and the stripes stopped chasing each other up the screen.

Okay, I'm slow. "The computer is going to make riddles?" I asked.

"Not exactly."

"What's that thing wired to the back of the terminal?" Long-Drink asked.

"A modem," Callahan said, and just then there were two sounds. My digital watch chirped, and the phone rang.

The big redheaded barkeep picked up the handset and put it down on the modem cradle. At once letters began to appear on the screen.

HI, FOLKS. I'M YOUR RIDDLEMASTER FOR THE NIGHT. MY NAME IS BILLY WALKER.

I could feel a big grin growing on the front of my face. "Mike, you Hibernian ham, you're a genius. Lemme at that keyboard."

He showed me how to use it, and I typed in HI, BILLY. MY NAME'S JAKE.

IT'S JAKE WITH ME IF IT'S JAKE WITH YOU, came the reply. I noticed that there was a pause about every tenth character, and realized that each pause represented a twitch.

OKAY, LET'S HAVE SOME RIDDLES. The whole gang was clustered around the monitor now, chattering and laughing; those who hadn't been around the night before last were being filled in.

YOU FOLKS READ SCIENCE FICTION, I UNDERSTAND?
Noah Gonzalez and I always did; as for the rest of the

crowd, well, somewhere between the second time-traveler and the third alien we got in Callahan's, most of them picked up on it too. YEAH.

HERE YOU GO, THEN, he replied, and the next lines appeared so rapidly he must have had them stored and ready.

> SCOTTISH MT.; FIDDLESTICK, ASSERT
> HYDROPHOBIC; Y'KNOW? (CAN.); DRUNK AND
> MENDACIOUS
> ORBS, FEH!; S. AMER. PALM, (COLOR OF ITS
> FRUIT)
> MARVEL COMICS; (QUIET!), GLOVE
> WASHROOM; CLONE YOURSELF; ECCENTRIC
> WHEEL, NONSENSE.

WHAT'S THE TOPIC? I asked him.

YOU TELL ME.

NOW I KNOW WHY THEY CALL IT A CURSOR.

Well, we all took turns chatting with Billy while we worked on his riddles, and it took us several hours to work out that the topic was "SF Writers" and that the answers were, in order,

"Ben; bow, aver" = Ben Bova

"Rabid; eh?; high 'n' lyin'" = Robert A. Heinlein

"Eyes, ech!; asa (mauve)" = Isaac Asimov

"Stan Lee; (shh!), mitt" = Stanley Schmidt

"John; double you; cam, bull" = John W. Campbell, and by that time Doc Webster had come up with the idea of Billy applying for a grant to start up a computer network for shut-ins, and we were all on the way to becoming good friends. Oh, once in a while I'd get a mental picture of the man on the other end of the hookup and giggle in spite of myself. But he never knew it. I've always hated that hairy old nonsense about high technology being inherently dehumanizing.

And as Doc Webster said, Billy's barks were much worse than his bytes.

CHAPTER 4

The Mick of Time

NEW YEAR'S EVE at Callahan's Place, and I was feeling about as much contentment as an unmarried man can know, thinking of how many New Year's Eves I'd spent in this warm, well-lit, cozy room with the best friends I'd ever known, thinking happily of how many more there would be to come. You'd think that would have warned me.

Somehow or other the conversation had turned to Conundra—the kind of questions that are good for keeping you entertained on an insomniac night, and not a whole lot else. They're sort of like test programs for the mind, and I guess New Year's Eve is a natural time for such things.

It was early on, not gone eight o'clock and only a handful of the regulars in attendance yet. Tommy Janssen had asked Long-Drink McGonnigle something, I forget what, and the Drink replied something along the lines of, "Son, that's one of those great Questions That Will Never Be Answered."

Doc Webster snorted. "Flapdoodle. Any meaningful question can be answered—and will be, sooner or later. Questions just never go away until they are."

Callahan finished reloading the coffeepot and came over to join us. "Doc," he rumbled, "if any question can be answered, maybe you can help me with one that's been occupyin' my mind for a long time now. How many angels can dance on the head of a beer?" There was a general giggle.

"I said, 'meaningful questions,'" the Doc replied. "Your question has no meaning because one of its crucial terms is undefined. Tell me—specifically—what you mean by an

105

'angel,' and I'll answer your question. Or rather, you'll have answered it yourself."

"Aw hell, Doc," Long-Drink said, "you know what an angel is."

"If I did, I wouldn't be paying alimony. My point is, it's easy to make up questions that don't have answers because they don't really ask anything. Can God make a rock so big he can't lift it? Where was Moses when the lights went out?"

"We're certainly into a theological vein here," said Tom Hauptmann, the former minister. "There's one that's always puzzled me, Doc, and I think it has meaning. Water is a clear, colorless fluid. So how come when you splash it on a towel, the towel gets darker?"

The Doc was silent for a moment, chewing on that, and Tommy and Long-Drink began to chuckle. "There's an answer," the Doc insisted. "I never said I knew all the answers—but if the question has meaning, the answer is knowable."

I thought of one that's kept my own mind harmlessly occupied for hours at a time. "Hey, Doc, I've got one. A thought-experiment, and a humdinger: It's one of those that causes a system-crash in the brain. The beauty of it is that one day soon it will be possible to try it out in the real world and *see* what the answer is—but right now, even though all the components of the question are meaningful and known, I'll bet a case of Anchor Steam Beer nobody here can come up with an answer and prove it."

"Hey," Susie Maser (Slippery Joe's senior wife) said, "for a case of all-barley beer, I'll take on Zeno's Paradox with one hand tied halfway behind my back. Whip it out, Jake." Several others leaned forward attentively.

"I've put this question to about thirty scientists in ten different disciplines," I said, "and to educators, and science fiction writers and editors I met at conventions, and the funny thing is that they all reacted the exact same way. I'd lay out the question, and they'd all start to answer right away . . . and then they'd catch themselves, and fall silent, and get a far look . . . and a minute or so later, they'd change the subject."

"Come on, come on," the Drink said. "Lay it on us."

"You're right," I said mournfully. "I'm taking too long to get to it. A man'll do that sometimes, when he's dehydrated—"

Long-Drink sighed and reached into his pants pocket. "Give the bastard a beer, Mike."

"Okay," I said when I'd blown the foam off and taken a sip, "this experiment could actually be done in sloppy form right now—but it purifies it a great deal if we imagine it taking place in space, in a microgravity environment. Let's say that somewhere up in orbit, there's a perfectly spherical object whose inner surface is mirrored: a spherical mirror, all right? Naturally, it's dark in there. Floating with his eyes at dead center is an astronaut—never mind how he got there," I said hastily as Susie began to object. "Maybe the mirror was blown around him; anyway, he's there. He's scared of the dark, so he takes a flashlight out of his pocket and turns it on. *What does he see?*"

Everyone in the room started to answer at once—

"Well, he—"

"The back of—"

"All of him at—"

"Nothing but pure white—"

—and then they all caught themselves. And fell silent. And got a far look.

After about ten seconds, Susie started to open her mouth. "Does it make any difference," I asked, "which way he points the flashlight? How would what he see change if he pointed the thing at himself? Or if he put it in his mouth and made Monster-Cheeks?" and Susie closed her mouth again.

When the silence had lasted for nearly a minute, Doc Webster said, "Another classic question I've always wanted to know the answer to is how and why evolution designed the human taste buds to love a poison like sugar."

I looked questioningly at Callahan, and he nodded. "Subject change," he agreed. "Appears to me that these birds owe you a case of Anchor Steam, Jake." He counted heads. "I make it a beer apiece; ante up, folks."

Grumbling, everybody did reach into their pockets, but they brightened considerably when Mike handed across my case and I started passing out the beers.

About that time Mick and Mary Finn came in, by the wrought-iron staircase from the roof. (Finn could just have easily landed on the ground, of course; the parking lot was still empty enough to make an excellent LZ—but he's had a sentimental attachment to that roof ever since the night he met his wife up there, and to the staircase since he married her on it, and he always comes in that way now.) There was a time when if Mickey came in, in the middle of a conversation, it had to sort of pause for a few minutes while we all helped him work his way into it. But marriage has, among the many other ways it's been good for the big alien, tended to humanize him a little, to make it easier for him to plug into things smoothly.

"Well, what do you know, it's a sawbuck!" I called out, and did not have to patiently explain to Finn that a sawbuck is two fins; he either got it or let it go. "Howdy, folks. Welcome to the feast of reason. The topic is Ponderable Questions—and the fine line between them and the imponderables. You two got any good ones?" I gave him a beer, and then I gave his wife a beer, and I don't even know why I bother mentioning that Mary smiled when I gave it to her, because the smile didn't do anything more than flay the skin off my body, sandblast every nerve and ligament, Osterize a few major organs and fry my eyeballs in their own grease; I made no visible sign that could possibly have been detected by anyone except the people present in the room. I'm over her completely.

"Certainly," Mickey said. "The more I live with humans, the more questions I have, and the more imponderable they become. Mary is better than any human I have ever known at explaining them—even better than you, Michael," he said to Callahan, "—but even she has no more than a sixty percent success rate."

"Ah, now we've hit pay-dirt," Doc Webster said. "What does an intelligent nonhuman think of the human race? We're such vain creatures it's one of the most fascinating questions we can imagine—spawned thousands of myths and books and movies."

"Well, naturally," Long-Drink agreed. "Man alone cannot know himself. The container can't contain itself."

Mickey Finn looked politely puzzled. "I do not understand what you mean. Do not all containers contain themselves? If not, what does contain them?"

The Drink got another far look. Finally the Doc said, "What puzzles you the most about humans, Mick? Politics? Sexual customs? Art? Philosophy?"

"Bathrooms," the big alien said at once.

"Jump *back*," Long-Drink said incredulously.

"I am serious, Drink, my friend," Finn told him. "I don't understand why *humans* are not puzzled by their bathrooms. I have wondered about this since before I quit working for my former Masters. I understand the concept of a blind-spot, but it is hard to comprehend one of this size."

"There's usually something substantial kinda blocking the view in that direction, Mickey," Callahan said dryly. "What exactly is it that puzzles you about bathrooms?"

"Everything, Michael. The first item one finds in a typical bathroom is the sink. I have made tests: half of the time and energy spent at a sink are used in adjusting water temperature. Your technology makes cheaply available thermocouples which will reliably deliver water of any specified temperature—yet in every single bathroom in the world the job is done by hand, with every use. Unbelievable waste of time and water and heated water.

"Next the medicine cabinet: I have never seen one designed with the intelligence of the average spice rack. You *have* to spill everything into the sink to access the aspirins.

"The human bathtub could only have been invented to help weed out the elderly, careless and unlucky; it could be argued that this is laudable, but why must even the survivors be made so *uncomfortable* during what ought to be a delightful chore? Why are comfortable head supports not standard; why must tubs always be too short, too narrow, too hard and too difficult to keep clean; why build them of such preposterous materials; and above all, why is the single shower-head almost invariably located where it cannot be brought to bear on the specific areas where it would be most useful and most pleasant?

"As for the commode . . . it would take a volume to simply list its gross deficiencies. Forget the insanity of throwing precious fecal matter into the ocean, along with gallons-per-bolus of drinking water—how could humans possibly have designed for daily use and accepted as a universal standard an artifact which is acutely physically painful to use, enforces an unnatural and inefficient posture, and has no facilities whatsoever for cleansing either its user or itself? And why do you persist in using them for male urinals though they are manifestly unsuitable for that purpose?

"To be fair, I must admit that given your level of technology there is not much to criticize in the towel rack—but my friends, from an engineering point of view it is the only pardonable object in a human bathroom."

Well, a few of us said a few things, but there's no sense kidding; Finn had us cold. It seemed strange that these things had never occurred to any of us before. Of course, we took bathrooms for granted, we'd grown up with them, but still . . .

About that time the door opened and a crisp breeze blew two men into the room; there was a glad shout as we recognized them.

"By all the Saints in Leslie Charteris's bookshelf," boomed Callahan, "if it ain't the MacDonald Brothers! About time you two bums showed up here. It's been too damn many years."

After a short merry interval of backslaps and handshakes and let-me-get-your-coats we got Jim and Paul seated at the bar with God's Blessings in front of them. "God, it's good to be back here," they chorused, and then Jim took over the vocalizing for both of them. "I make it three years," he said to Callahan, and, "Yes, Jake, two years ago, and yes,

it is," to me, and "Upstate in Plattsburgh—and it's getting
pretty sane there," to Long-Drink, and "Perfect, thanks;
we're learning some things about repairing ourselves," to
Doc Webster, and, "No, Eddie—we don't need one," to
Fast Eddie, and, "No, Reverend, and don't think we haven't
tried," to Tom Hauptmann, and then, to all of us: "We're
sorry, we ought to let you vocalize the questions so you can
all share the answers—but there were so many in the first
round that we wanted to save a little time."

Jim and Paul are telepaths, you see.* What I'd been
wondering was if they'd finished getting certified as psychiatrists yet, and if so whether it was working out the way
they'd hoped. Some of the others' questions I could puzzle
out. Callahan had been wondering how long it's been since
their last visit; the Drink was going to ask where they were
practicing; the Doc was going to ask after their health.
Eddie's and Tom's questions eluded me.

"Hello, Mary," Jim went on, "it's good to meet you, too.
God, what a lovely marriage you two have! No, really? But
that's *wonderful!* Don't worry, we wouldn't dream of it.
Thanks. Finn, that's really fascinating stuff about the human
bathroom. Do you see a pattern? Do the rest of you?" I'd
been thinking of filling Jim and Paul in on the conversation
that'd been in progress when they arrived, but of course
they were a step ahead of me. "Consider: the same inherent
stupidity Finn points out can be found in the typical kitchen.
Fridges that spill money on the floor when you access them;
stoves and ovens that spill money on the ceiling; a heat-
maker and a heat-waster side by side, unconnected; sinks
with the same problems he mentioned and others; waste-
management techniques that belong in the Stone Age.

"In the typical bedroom you'll find just as much inexplicable thoughtlessness. It's only in the last year or two
that anyone even thought of adapting hospital-bed technology to home beds. The three rooms all people *must* spend

*see "Two Heads Are Better Than One," in CALLAHAN'S CROSSTIME SALOON
(Berkley).

time in every day, none of them rationally designed. Yet in the den you'll probably find a computer that's a masterpiece of skullsweat and micromachining, and overhead there are satellites beeping in high orbit and footprints on the Moon. Right now Paul and I are planning to spend over a thousand dollars on a hard-disk drive for our Macintosh, because it drives us crazy having to wait more than seven seconds to boot in, and it never occurred to either of us to spend fifty dollars on a thermocouple to save us hours a week of adjusting hot and cold water taps. Humans seem to have the idea that it's okay to devote thought and money and energy to our jobs, but not to our selves."

He paused courteously to let Doc Webster say aloud, "I don't know; we indulge ourselves pretty good in some ways. They make some pretty fancy entertainment gear, stereo and video and computer games and so forth."

"Nothing near as fancy as the stuff people use for work. In our Mac Buyer's Guide, business applications programs outnumber software games ten or twenty to one. All the stuff you mention was used for work for years before they made home consumer versions. And you can't sit in anything *near* as comfortable as a dentist's chair to enjoy them all. Holdover of the Puritan ethic: work can be noble, but the self is not worth attention. Considering that useful work is getting harder to come by, it's an attitude we're going to have to change eventually."

"I dunno," Doc Webster said. "I think we put in plenty of time on enjoyin' ourselves; maybe too much."

"Maybe. But I think we enjoy ourselves in inappropriate ways, at inappropriate times, to inappropriate degrees, just *because* we're so unused to doing it, so uncomfortable with wanting to, so reluctant to put thought into it. Paul and I find that most of our patients don't love themselves enough, so they treat themselves so badly it's hard for them to love themselves enough—it can be a literally vicious circle."

Finn glanced at Mary on that one, and she smiled fondly. "See, kid? It's not just a human problem, is it?" He smiled sheepishly back. "Don't worry, you're making progress." She turned back to the MacDonald brothers. "I'm glad to meet you fellows, and you've got a mighty insight going there, which come to think of it is no surprise, but... *can we tell it now?* You know I'm dying to."

Jim and Paul both smiled, and this time it was Paul who did their talking. "Of course, dear. I don't know how you've held it in this long. Go ahead."

She turned to the rest of us. "You folks know what's been keeping Mick awake nights since he got to this planet, right?"

"Sure," Tommy Janssen said. "Same thing that keeps a lot of us human type beings awake nights too."

"And I don't know about the rest of you," the Doc insisted on saying, "but Armageddon awful tired of it."

Mary ignored him magnificently. "That's right: nuclear holocaust. It wouldn't bother him any, physically, of course— and by the way, it wouldn't bother me or any of you physically either. You know how raindrops ignore friends of Mick's? Well, ionizing radiation and blast forces behave the same way, now." She reached over the bar, took out Callahan's riot-baton, and brought it down on my head as hard as she could. A microinstant after it struck, the top of my head turned hard as titanium alloy.

"That's fantastic," I said as soon as I could get my breath. "I felt a little sting, as though you slapped me with your open palm."

"That's the most pain you'd feel even if I shot you with Pop's 12-gauge," she said, grinning broadly. "However you die, Jake, it won't be by violence. But that's beside the point. Nuclear devastation would be a sad thing even for us who survived. We'd miss the rest of the human race—"

"Speak for yourself," the Doc interjected.

"—and as for Mick, without a high-tech civilization, he'd die in a few hundred years for lack of maintenance. So he and I have been working on the problem ever since we got married, kind of putting our heads together, and the reason we came here tonight is—"

"To kick around some ideas, sure," Tommy said. "Great. As long as we're all brainstorming the Unanswerable Questions, we might as well tackle the Big One."

"Well, no, actually," Mary said. "I mean, we'd be glad to kick around ideas on some other topics with you later, if you like. But this one we've sort of ... uh ... solved."

"WHAT?"

I let go of my drink; Long-Drink started so sharply his watchman's cap flew from his head; Tommy spit a cigarette across the room; Fast Eddie the piano player had what musicians call a "train wreck"; the Doc was caught without a wisecrack of any kind; and Callahan—imperturbable Callahan—poured coffee on his hand and let out a bellow. It is worth mentioning that my drink didn't go anywhere, the Drink's cap returned to its perch, Tommy's cigarette landed in wet sawdust and extinguished itself, the Doc's flabby old heart did not stop, and the coffee failed to burn Callahan's wrist. The MacDonald Brothers were grinning a mile a minute, and even Finn had a happy expression pasted on his long gaunt face. Mary looked more embarrassed than anything else, like someone who's solved the whole crossword in two minutes and spoiled everyone's fun. *Jake,* I thought to myself, taking hold of my glass again, *you sure can pick 'em.* It seemed astonishing that I had ever thought myself this woman's equal, imagined us living together ... (It's stupid to be jealous of someone with Mickey Finn's unique advantages, especially when he's such a good friend. But I had learned lately that I'm easily that stupid.)

None of us doubted her for a moment, of course. In the first place this was Callahan's Bar, where *anything* can happen—and frequently does; in the second place, she was Mike Callahan's daughter, and therefore capable of anything she put her mind to; in the last place, she was Finn's wife. Me, I gave up using the word "impossible" after the time I watched Fast Eddie win a large bet by successfully skiing through a revolving door. If Mary Callahan Finn said nuclear war wasn't a problem anymore, then it was time to start converting my fallout shelter back into a root cellar again, that was all ...

The tone of Callahan's voice, now there was something

genuinely startling. "Darlin'," he said darkly, "I would like to know, if you wouldn't mind telling me, exactly *how* you and Mick solved this little problem."

"No, Mike, no," Jim or Paul hastened to assure him. "Nothing like that."

Mary apparently knew her old man well enough to read him as well as two professional telepaths. "You ought to know me better than that, Pop. No—to answer your question out loud for everyone else's benefit—we did *not* solve the problem of nuclear war by making any changes in human nature. I'm not saying Mick couldn't pull it off if he tried, with enough lead time, but he wouldn't. Besides, I wouldn't let him. The very aggressiveness that makes the human race dangerous to itself is what's going to take us to the stars one of these days—you couldn't filter it out without changing humanity for the worse, maybe destroying it."

"My own race lacked that sort of aggressiveness," Finn put in. "I am its last living member, and it has not escaped me that there may be a connection. I am more advanced, more knowledgeable than any of you—and even I am not competent to alter a psyche, individual or collective, Michael."

Callahan relaxed. "Well, that's okay then. I misgive my misgivings. Irish Coffee, anybody?"

Long-Drink exploded. *"How did you fucking do it?"*

"Well," Mary said, "you all have to promise not to tell a soul—anybody that isn't a regular, I mean..."

She was cut off by the sound of the blender as Callahan whipped cream for the Irish coffee. The big red-headed son of a bitch made us wait on eleventerhooks until he was done, had Mary hold off until he had Blessed everyone in the room, then waved her to go ahead. Jim and Paul were smiling their faces off. I took a deep gulp of my own black magic healing potion, and decided that Callahan had good instincts and a nice judgment.

"You all know," she said, "that Mick and I have been spending our honeymoon traveling. I'd always wanted to see the world, and what with one thing and another I'd never managed to find the time to visit more than a dozen countries or so. So Mick indulged me. You know, it's funny how fast you can use up the tourist attractions of this planet when none of your time is wasted in the fiddle-faddle of getting there, and hauling and storing your stuff, and eating and drinking, and all of that chaff. On top of that, I hardly ever sleep since I took up with Mick—I don't *need* to anymore, and it makes me feel a little silly and selfish to go off and leave him for eight hours at a time like that. So in an astonishingly short time I discovered I was bored and there was nothing left to see.

"Well, you all know how polite this big cyborg is, but eventually he broke down and managed to diffidently suggest that Terra is *not* the only or even the most beautiful tourist attraction in this solar system.

"You want to know the truth, people? It's not even in the Top Ten...

"So lately we've been doing some *real* traveling, having a wonderful time. One day we were hanging out in The Rings—"

"Saturn?" I burst out.

"I *said* it with a capital T, Jake. Hanging out in The Rings, just sort of digging, you know, and chewing the fat now and then. We talked about the Cockroaches" (the name Mary came up with for Finn's former employers when she could not bring herself to call them The Masters) "and some of the other planets and civilizations he's seen, and so forth. And of course Topic A kept coming up—you just can't look at a sterile planet for long without thinking about it—and all of a sudden Finn asked me a question."

Just like a human husband, Finn interpreted her pause and took up the tale. She's had a considerable effect on him. "The news had been full of the Disarmament Talks when we left; you will recall that the Russians refused to even discuss the subject unless Reagan promised to abort his plans for a defensive satellite network—"

"Oh," said Long-Drink, "you mean the Star W—" Callahan hefted the big fifteen-cup coffee pot in one hand like a set of brass knuckles. "—the Strategic Defense Initiative, sure," the Drink finished.

"Yes," Finn agreed. "I asked Mary: why does not Reagan say to Gorbachev, 'Let us mutually agree to found together, in a neutral country such as Switzerland or New Zealand, *a single factory* which manufactures defensive satellites; divide the inventory at random; and launch them two by two until each side feels safe. Until that time is reached, each of us shall have a button which will destroy the factory if he suspects the other is cheating in any way. In that way—"

"If the Russians could build them things on their own, they'd be doing it," Long-Drink said argumentatively. "The U.S.'d contribute a lot more to the party than the Russians."

"So what?" Finn said simply.

The Drink opened his mouth. After a moment he reached up and closed it with his fingers.

"So what'd you answer, darlin'?" Callahan asked his daughter.

"I told him that it wouldn't work, but I couldn't explain why not. He said that was his thinking, too; just checking. But it gave me a honey of an idea—"

"I am ashamed that I never thought of it myself," Finn said. "It is so obvious—"

"My love," she told him, "from a human's perspective there are only two deficiencies in your character: aggressiveness, as we discussed before, and audacity." *And a sense of humor,* I thought jealously, and suppressed the thought. Funny how you start censoring yourself when there's a couple of telepaths in the room. "But not imagination. Once I laid it down, you picked it up and ran with it." She turned back to the rest of us. "Mick's thoughts had been along the lines of figuring out some way to destroy nuclear warheads, and of course the problem was that even he couldn't get all of them simultaneously—and anything less would probably *trigger* a nuclear exchange. Even if he managed it, he might have just kicked off a conventional war that'd be damn near as bad. Well, it occurred to me that a satellite umbrella system would make the nut just fine, except that neither side wants the other to have one *first,* and they're too damn paranoid to coordinate or synchronize with each other.

"So Mick and I decided to do it for them."

After a frozen second or two, people began to grin along with Jim and Paul.

"We ducked over to the Asteroid Belt for raw materials, Finn drew up the blueprints and I set up a smithy, and we started turning out defensive satellites, free-lance. A little more sophisticated than the ones Reagan's advisors have in mind. They're in place now; we just hung the last one an hour or two ago."

Callahan frowned. "You sure nobody caught you at it?"

"Relax, Mike," she told him. "Nobody sees Mick, on any wavelength whatsoever, unless he wants them to. As for the hardware, the largest components, the four system brains, are the size of ghetto blasters—and as transparent as glass. You could *tell* NASA roughly where they are, and give them twenty years, and they'd never find 'em.

"But for gosh sakes, don't tell anybody," Mary went on. "A general tends to freak out when he finds out his dick won't shoot. Of course, if they're dumb enough to let the situation, uh, come up, then the hell with their feelings—but for now, let's leave them with the comforting illusion that they hold the fate of mammalian life in their hands—it'll keep 'em out of serious mischief."

A rebel yell went up from someone, and like the first firecracker in a string it kicked off the loudest, and happiest, and most sincere cheer I had ever participated in or heard of in my life. It started loud, and built to a crescendo, and then squared itself, and then sustained, and eventually, there being a limit to the capacity of human lungs, dwindled, dopplered down, attenuated and finally was reduced to a single voice. And, astonishingly, the voice was very soft, very quiet, very flat, almost totally devoid of any emotion at all. It was an oddly chilling effect. *Oh, for heaven's sake, I told myself, it's just that it's Finn, and he forgets to put expression into his voice sometimes,* and as my blood started to unchill it froze solid because I heard what he was murmuring so gently, over and over:

"I have made a terrible mistake."

What made it even more horrible was that Jim and Paul MacDonald, dumbstruck, were nodding along with him.

Mary's face paled; I think if both her parents had been Caucasian she would have been white as a sheet. "What *is* it, Mick? What's wrong, for Christ's sake? I thought about it for weeks, you thought about it for hours, *what did we miss?*"

If anyone could have reached Finn it was Mary, but he didn't seem to hear her. She shook him, kicked him in the shin, and beat a tattoo on his face with her fists, without attracting his attention; he was a tall thin juke-box with a stuck record, repeating over and over again, "I have made a terrible mistake."

"Jim," Callahan said sharply, "what's wrong with him?"

But it was older brother Paul who answered. "The same thing that was wrong with me the first night my brother came in here, Mike. He's mindblown."

"Damn straight," Tommy Janssen said. "But what by?"

"We'll get to that," Callahan said. "First of all, how do we get him out of it before he wears a groove into his brain?"

"It won't be easy," Paul said. "When something scares you shitless, you just go back up inside your head and hide. But when the thing that scares you *comes* from inside your head, you . . . well, you go to a place that isn't a place, erasing your footsteps behind you. It'll be hard to find him: even he doesn't know where he is right now."

"I can get him back," Mary said positively.

I halfway expected her to borrow Callahan's scattergun and shoot Mick in the head—it seemed like a reasonable idea; it couldn't hurt him or anything—but what she did was, if you think about it, even more dramatic.

She leaned close to him and said, quietly but clearly over the sound of his litany, "Mick, I need you."

"Yes, Mary." His eyeballs powered up, tracked her, and locked on.

"Standby mode, sweetheart. I'll reboot you when it's time."

"Yes, dear." His face smoothed over and he turned to stone.

"Nice job, Mary," Paul said.

"Oh, shit," she said, "the *job* hasn't started yet. Before I start him up again, I've got to have his universe rebuilt for him, or he'll just split again. So start talking: what's his problem?"

"Oh, it's ours, too," he assured her, "and it's a beaut. Finn's Masters just entered the fringes of the cometary zone. They're headed this way."

"The fucking Cockroaches," Mary whispered, and literally pissed her pants. She glanced down at the widening stain on her jeans, smiled, and Paul and Jim caught her as she started to fall. She's so big it's a good thing there were two of them, but they got her down gently. She was out cold. Neither Mike nor I had even started to move to help her.

"Oh, spiffing!" Jim said. "Two down, one dozen to go."

He was paraphrasing a mordantly funny *Fawlty Towers* episode known to every one of us in the room, in a very good imitation of John Cleese's voice, and it may sound horrible but it was the most perfect way I can imagine to reach all of us, keep *us* from going bugfuck, too. Nobody cracked up, but nobody cracked up either, if you follow.

"But it's impossible!" I burst out. "He said they wouldn't—they're cowards—he said they'd write him off when he failed to report—"

"Wishful thinking, maybe," Callahan said softly.

Paul and Jim shook their heads. "No, Mike," Jim said. "To the best of Finn's knowledge, what's happening is unlikely to the point of impossibility. He can't account for it. There's got to be something he doesn't know about the situation. My own suspicion is that he's not as expendable as the Cockroaches told him he was, for some reason, but that's just a hunch. In any case, they're on the way."

"Do they know that Mickey's here?" Callahan asked.

Jesus—if they did, they were on their way to *this room*.

"Not yet," Jim replied. "But they will, soon. Finn's expecting to hear the call any minute: *'Report!'* When it comes, he'll answer it. Nothing in the world he can do about it."

"Not even in that condition?" Callahan asked, gesturing toward the catatonic Finn.

"He's not capable of ignoring a direct command from a Master: he's counterprogrammed. That's why he needed you folks to help him, that first night he walked in here."

"No sweat, then," Callahan said, and reached under the bar for the chloral hydrate. "We'll just slip him another shot of his namesake." It happens that chloral hydrate is one of the very few things that affect Finn exactly the same way they do a human: it is about the only thing that can render him truly unconscious.

"It's not that simple. Mary put him on standby—"

"So we pry his mouth open and pour the stuff down his throat—"

"Mike, in this mode, his stomach won't uptake."

"Oh. Well, can you power him back up again?"

"We'll have to wake Mary up: she's the only Authorized User inside the orbit of Neptune. Give us some silence, people. She's had a shock; it's going to be hard to do this without damaging her . . ."

We shut up and let them work. After maybe five long silent seconds, Mary opened her eyes and sat up. "We'll have to hurry," she said, "the Roaches could jerk his chain any second now." She got to her feet quickly enough to surprise even me, who have reason to know how limber she is. Obviously Jim and Paul had brought her up to date in the process of waking her. "It's time to get up, darling."

The statue of Finn came to life. The eyes started to smolder.

"Don't worry, now," she said quickly. "Open your mouth and drink what I give you."

"Yes, Mary."

Without taking her eyes from him she held up her hand, and the little bottle of chloral hydrate that Callahan tossed landed squarely in it. (I thought of my own father, and Mount Washington, and a hat.) "About thirty cc's," he called, and she beheaded the bottle and poured the dosage past her husband's teeth. Fast Eddie and Long-Drink and I were alert; we reached Finn in time to help Mary and the MacDonalds break his fall. Finn's more than six-eleven, but thinner than me; he looks and moves like he weighs less than his wife. But this was the second time I'd helped carry him, and I'd guess him at six hundred pounds or better. Lead in the alloy? A grain of neutronium? I'd always meant to ask. We laid him out near where Mary had been a moment ago, straightened up and rubbed our kidneys.

"Well," Long-Drink rumbled, "everything's fine, now. Finn's the most powerful critter that ever walked the earth, and the people who scare the crap out of *him* are on the way to exterminate us, and we've successfully put out the lights of the only guy who might have any ideas. Anybody feel like playing darts?"

"We've still got Finn, in a sense," I said. "Jim-Paul, you took a reading on him."

"All we've got is data," Paul answered for them. "Not the metaprogrammer part, the part that generates ideas and thinks ten times faster than a human." He looked helpless. "And not much of the data, either. We've never been able to read more than about fifty percent of Finn's mind, and we only got maybe the surface five percent of that—a human brain just doesn't have the storage capacity, Jake. Not even two human brains."

"Mike," Long-Drink McGonnigle said hollowly, "drinks for the house, on me."

Do you know, I had room left in my brain to be startled by that? Of course, I realized at once, he was going to put it on his tab . . .

"Did you get a reading on how soon the Cockroaches will get here?" Mary asked as Callahan began passing out fresh booze. "And what'll happen when they do?"

"They'll check Mars first, then come here; they should reach high orbit in an hour or so. Not having heard any response from Finn, the first thing they'll do is to scan the planet for clues to his fate. If they don't find any, they'll sterilize Earth and go on to check out Venus—then when they don't find him there either, I guess they'll—"

Fast Eddie spoke up from his place on the piano bunch. "I don't t'ink I give a shit what dey do after dey sterilize de Oyth, Paulie."

He sighed. "I don't suppose I do either, Ed."

"What happens if they *do* find Finn?" Callahan asked.

"If he wakes up between now and then, you mean? Why, I guess they'd come here and look him over, find out what caused him to malfunction and see if he could be restored to service. *Then* they'd sterilize Earth—probably have Mickey do it for them, to make sure he was working properly again."

"How many of 'em do you figure there are?"

Both MacDonalds shrugged. "Impossible to say, Mike. Finn couldn't come up with a reason why *any* of them would come here."

"Are they vulnerable to anything?"

"Oh, yes. If they were as strong as Finn, they wouldn't need scouts like Finn. That's why he can't imagine what would bring them here; he's certain there are no other scouts along with them. Anyway, all you'd have to do is detonate a small tactical nuke in their immediate vicinity and you'd have Cockroach Soup."

"Well, hell," Doc Webster said, "NORAD can handle that! With Finn to spot for 'em, maybe..." He trailed off as it dawned on him. "Aw, shit."

"NORAD doesn't have any H-bombs anymore," Callahan rumbled. "Mick *said* he made a terrible mistake."

Mary buried her face in her hands. "Oh, Pop! *I made it, too!*" She began to sob.

I wanted to rush to her and comfort her, take her in my arms and tell her everything was going to be all right. I never moved a muscle and I never said a mumbling word.

Her father came around the bar and put an arm around

her. "So did I, darlin', so did I. Not your fault. We guessed wrong, that's all."

"Pop, what'll we do now?"

"I'm not exactly certain, hon, but the first step is to blow our cover."

Her head came up fast. "Are you *sure?*"

The big barkeep grinned at her, waggled his cigar. "Hell, no! Got a better idea?"

She frowned. "I guess not. Your privilege; they're your family."

Callahan turned to the rest of us. "Folks, I'm afraid it's time for Mary and I to face the music, and tell you people who we really are . . ."

And having said that much, the big red-headed son of a bitch stood there and looked at us for a while. He's always had a pretty expressive face, but I'd never seen so many expressions chase themselves around it before. And while I've always known that Michael Callahan was a subtle and thoughtful man, I'd known it by his actions more than his face; his expressions had always been sort of carved out in broad strokes before. This was a change so sharp as to be perceptible. Somehow I knew that I was looking at a different man. No: at a different side of a man I knew. It was something like watching a brilliant actor step out of character after the lights have gone out.

It was exactly like that. I began to add up a number of things that I have always known but somehow had never felt inclined to think about for very long. Not, say, for long enough to reach the inevitable conclusions.

I glanced toward the MacDonalds. Jim's eyes were waiting for mine, and he was nodding. I opened my mouth . . . then shut up and let Callahan say it.

"Friends," he said slowly, "this isn't going to be easy. A lot of words I need, I don't have. Not that they don't exist, but none of you know 'em—and I don't have time for a language lesson. Uh . . . Mary and I aren't from around here—"

"We know that, Mike," Long-Drink said. "Brooklyn, right?"

"Dat's where me and Mike hooked up," agreed Eddie, the oldest denizen of Callahan's Place. "At Sally's joint."

Callahan shook his head. "That ain't where I'm from, boys."

Eddie shrugged. "Well, you never said it was."

"Thanks, Eddie." Callahan smiled at the monkey-faced little piano man. "I'm pleased you noticed that."

"All right," Doc Webster said. "I'll play. Where *are* you from?"

"A place that calls itself Harmony."

"Isn't that in New Zealand?" somebody asked.

"Nope. It's about twenty billion miles further away, and quite a few years from now."

There was silence for a time. Mary sat down at the nearest table and commandeered someone's neglected drink. She watched Finn snore while she sipped it.

"Well," Doc Webster said finally in a conversational tone, "that explains a lot. Always said there was something weird about you, Callahan. Anyone who would permit puns like mine in his establishment is just not normal."

"Time traveler, huh?" Tommy Janssen mused. "You must be from further up the line than The Meddler or Al Phee."

"Or Josie Bauer and her Time-Police,*" Callahan agreed. "To my time, yours and theirs are pretty much indistinguishable."

"How far is that, Mike?" I asked.

"Well," he said, "where I come from, the human race has got it together. Nobody's hungry; nobody's angry."

That far!

"And we're startin' to learn a few things. Oh, we'll be a *long* time learning—but at least we're finally on the case."

"Jesus Christ," I said faintly, "I wish I had time to ask you about five hundred questions."

*see "Have You Heard The One . . . ?" in TIME TRAVELERS STRICTLY CASH (Ace).

"Me too, Jake," he said. "But I'll tell you right now, better'n half of them I'd never be able to answer, in any words that'd have meaning for you. Like, right now, most of you are probably wondering about time paradoxes and so forth, and the answers simply won't mean much to you."

"Let's try anyway," Doc Webster said. "Did you know this showdown with Finn's Masters was gonna happen? Is that why you've been running this bar all these years?"

"Yes and no," Callahan said promptly. "See what I mean?"

"Dammit," the Doc growled, "I started out this night saying that all questions have answers."

"If they're meaningful," Callahan agreed. "Doc, you just plain can't frame a meaningful question about time-travel in English. The language itself hasn't got the room: it's based on the assumption that time-travel is not possible."

The Doc frowned. "So it is. Can you do any better than 'yes and no'?"

"It is known in my time that *some* event takes place at this locus in space/time. Something so major, so crucial to the history that produced my time, that it makes Pearl Harbor seem no more important than yesterday's hockey scores. What that event is, is hidden from us. So is the certainty of its outcome. Some things in our past we can't affect. Some things we *have to* affect. We don't always know the difference. And no, that's not the only reason I set up this bar, although it would have been enough. I know all that doesn't make sense, in English, but if you want me to do even a little better than that, we'll still be talking when the Cockroaches get here."

Good point. "All right," I said, "let's cut to the chase. You've got to have some kind of futuristic wonder-gizmo you can zap the Cockroaches with, right?"

I don't know when I've ever been sorrier to see a man shake his head. "It doesn't work that way, Jake. You have to work with available materials. Whatever's already in place in that space/time."

"Mike—," I hesitated. "If it was anybody but you, I'd say that was preposterous. How do you get your own time machine through?"

"We don't use machines for time-travel."

"Oh." I would think about this another time. If there ever was one. "But in any case we can relax, no? At least a little? The fact that you're here, from our future, means that the human race is *not* going to be exterminated in the next hour, *nicht wahr?* But we could suffer heavy casualties or something?"

That was when I've been sorrier to see a man shake his head. "Again, Jake, what you're saying sounds logical—because you're saying it in English. Take my word for it: my home space/time is just as likely as yours to stop existing in the next hour or so. Worse, to stop ever *having existed* in this continuum. If the Cockroaches steam-clean this planet, there'll be no way for my home to ever come to pass." He frowned. "This whole era is a tinder-box; we've got agents spotted all through here/now, doing what we can to cool things out. But we always knew that there was going to be at least one really major something around about now. What we *thought* was that the crucial event in question would be a nuclear firestorm. The shape of history seemed to point that way. We thought we had it covered, thanks to Finn." He looked sadly at his catatonic friend. "But it was us made the awful mistake, not him."

Long-Drink McGonnigle summed it up very succinctly, I thought: "Aw, shit."

"Don't feel bad, Mike," I said. "You bet with the odds—nobody can fault you for using Occam's Razor."

He shook his head ruefully. "Thanks, Jake—but you'd be surprised how many chins William can't shave. With the stakes this high, we should never have bet the farm."

"William who?" Fast Eddie wanted to know. "And what's dis about razors?"

That almost made me smile. Eddie must use an electric razor with an offset shim: at all times, he has exactly three days' growth of beard. "William of Occam, Eddie. Stated the principle of Least Hypothesis—"

"Is dat, like, cheaper than a rented hypot'esis?"

Bless the runty little piano man, that *did* make me smile, and simplify my explanation even further than I had planned.

"Occam's Razor is a principle that says, if there's more than one explanation for something, the simplest one is most likely to be true."

"Not 'certain,'" Callahan amplified. "'Most likely.'"

Eddie looked thoughtful—not an easy trick with that face—and shook his head. "I dunno. Most o' my life, de complicated explanation was de one to bet on. I don't buy dis William o' Whatever—"

"Occam," I said.

"—an' de horse he rode in on," Eddie agreed. "He sure got it wrong dis time." He frowned slightly at our grins. "Well, what's our next move, boss?"

The grins went away.

"Mike!" I said as an urgent thought struck me. "It's New Year's Eve! The rest of the gang are going to start showing up any second—all of 'em, not just the regulars. Shouldn't we try to head 'em off? Go set up roadblocks? *Some*thing?"

He took one of those foul cigars of his from a shirt pocket and sniffed it meditatively. What more proof did I need that he wasn't a normal human being? "I don't think so, Jake. In the immortal words of Percy Mayfield—"

"—'The Danger Zone is *everywhere*,' yeah, I understand that. They're no safer at home than they would be here. But do we want 'em all around underfoot, complicating the fight?" I felt my voice get hoarser. "There's going to be a fight here, isn't there?"

He lit his cigar. "Damn straight there is," he rumbled. He dropped the dead match on the floor, trod it underfoot, and took Mary's hand. "Damn straight." Suddenly he grinned. "But who ever said a fight was complicated by reinforcements? Let 'em come, by Christ. Let 'em all come! If we have to, we can all go to Hell together—maybe there's a group rate."

"Callahan's right, Jake," Long-Drink said. "There ain't a one of the gang wouldn't rather be *here* on Judgment Day, and you know it."

Doc Webster nodded vigorous agreement, jowls flapping. "Damn well told. If the world is about to end, we can at least have a drink on it together before we go!"

There was a general chorus of agreement.

"All right," Callahan boomed, "let's get to it. There's two phone lines in this joint, and the one for the computer is miked. I'll boot the directory disk and get a printout by last name—I'll take A through M; Doc, you take N through Z—"

"Mike," Jim and Paul MacDonald said simultaneously.

He broke off and tried to look at both at once. "Yeah?"

"It's not necessary to use the phone," they chorused.

He looked startled—then broke into a big grin. "Why, no, it ain't at that. What's your range these days?"

"With *family?* Callahan's People? We could find one of you on the Moon if we had to."

"Go to it then, sons."

Jim and Paul found a vacant table, sat down on opposite sides. They took each other's hands and smiled at one another. Then their eyes rolled up and their mouths went slack and they seemed to slump slightly.

Can you remember the very first time you used stereo headphones, and heard a voice speaking or singing *inside* your head? Or were you too young at the time to find that remarkable? This was a little like that: perceiving "sound" where sound had never been before.

(Further: You know that with stereo headphones an aural image can seem to move, from left to right or the other way around. In the Decca, Georg Solti recording of Wagner's *Der Ring des Niebelungen* there's a passage in which Fafnir roars—and on headphones the sound seems to move *up* from your throat to the crown of your head. An illusion, of course, and I've always wondered how Decca's engineers managed it. Similarly—and just as impossibly—the combined "voice" of Jim and Paul MacDonald, which I heard now in my head, seemed to move *from back to front,* as though two tiny Paul Reveres entered the back of my skull, transited my brain at high speed, and left through my forehead.)

The double-tracked voice was quiet, calm—but so emphatically urgent that I was certain it would have waked me out of the soundest sleep.

"**Mike Callahan needs you**," it said. "**Hurry!**"

The cold winter wind was choppy at this height, and the ledge was slippery; Walter clutched at the brick facade with slowly numbing fingers and at the pretty brunette's gaze with tearing eyes. She was nice to look at, leaning out the window, the last pretty girl he ever expected to see—but he knew all the things she was likely to say, and knew that none of them would work. "You're wasting your time," he told her and her husband, whose head was visible beside hers. "I know all the clichés, and I just don't want to talk about it."

"You've got to come in soon, Walter," she called from the window. "If you stay there much longer you'll get Window-Washer's VD."

"What?" To be surprised astonished him.

"It's a terrible thing," her husband said earnestly. "You get a watery blue discharge, with a funny smell."

"What the *hell* are you talking about?"

"Herpes windex," she said.

He laughed long and hard, to a point just short of hysteria. "You two really are good at what you do, you know that? I was in a lousy mood. This is a better mood to die in."

"That's something, at least," the husband called over the sound of the wind. "But—"

"I still don't want to talk about it," Walter yelled. "Why I'm doing this is none of your business."

"Nobody asked you," the wife said. "What Les and I want to know is why you're doing it so badly."

He blinked at them.

"Merry's right. Some janitor has to mop up you and his breakfast; a bunch of cops and ambulance attendants get brought down; a whole street-full of passersby have a great dark demoralizing omen literally drop into their lives—see that little girl across the street down there? Her mother is the one who's going to need to explain this, not us."

"And what *about* us?" Merry asked. "We're professionals, with a reputation to protect. You hired us to come over here and try to cheer you up. You say we succeeded, and now you want to skip out without paying. Are we supposed to—" She broke off short.

"You don't understand!" Walter shouted to the night sky. He closed his eyes, and sighed deeply. If he told them how it was, they would see that he really had no choice. "All right: I'll explain it to you. You deserve that much." He turned his face back to them, to see the empathy he knew he would find in Merry's eyes, and she and Les were both gone from the window. "Hey! Do you want to hear this or not?" There was no reply. *"Hey!"*

The Cheerful Charlies were gone.

Walter stood there on the ledge, confused, unready to jump, too stiff and cold to risk climbing back in the window unassisted, his scenario thrown completely off the rails. Anger came to him, bringing warmth to his fingers and strength to his limbs. He made it safely inside, and reached the street in time to see the Charlies driving away; furious, he flagged a cab and followed them.

Patrolman Jimmy Wyzniak trailed the Sergeant through the empty corridors of Suffolk County Police Headquarters; the only sounds were their footsteps and the occasional ringing of phones that no one was going to answer. Jimmy was young, and just barely experienced enough at his job to have some appreciation of the magnitude of his ignorance, but he had no fear: his Sergeant was with him, and the Sarge was the best there was. It had been bravery and not bad judgment that lost him a leg.

"People are sure funny, you know?" Jimmy said plaintively. "I mean, Captain Whitfield is taking this like it was personal—like they put it here just for him. Never seen him so mad."

The Sarge spoke over his shoulder. "You notice he didn't try to do the damned thing himself first. He called for the experts." His limp was barely perceptible.

Jimmy shifted his trunk-shield like an umpire looking for a fresh plug of tobacco and grinned. "Well, that just proves he's smarter than we are."

His mentor snorted. "Son, *everyone* is smarter than we are. Here we go: Storage Closet 5. The phone tip said it was in here."

"Who claimed credit for this one?"

"Who cares?"

"Boobies on the door, you figure?"

"Never can tell—so we assume there are." Jimmy set down the heavy backpack of equipment, and they spent a few minutes assuring themselves that the door was *not* booby-trapped. "I hope they're professionals," the Sarge grunted. "Pros are tricky sometimes—but at least they use good equipment. An amateur job, who knows *what* the hell it's gonna do?" Then, rank having its "privileges," the Sarge sent Jimmy thirty feet down the hall and around a corner. The young patrolman waited anxiously, heard the sound of the sarge trying the knob.

"Zoroaster in lingerie," he heard the Sarge say.

He ran back and looked through the door of Closet 5. "What the hell is it?" he asked. "That doesn't look like anything we covered in training."

"*I* saw one once," the Sarge said very softly. "When I was in the Army. I'd guess it's not especially powerful— nothing like the one that did that slum clearance on downtown Nagasaki. By today's military standards it's not even a cherry bomb."

Jimmy regarded the object. "You're saying that's a nuke," he said in a calm, conversational tone, as though confirming the time—then, big: "*It looks like a fucking miniature vacuum cleaner!*"

"Sure does—probably doesn't weigh more than thirty pounds all told. Now, the military could make one that size with some real bang onto it—but looky there at the airline bag they carried it in. Amateur job."

It was not machismo that kept Jimmy's cool for him— this was beyond even the machismo of a demolitions man.

But if the Sarge wasn't worried, Jimmy wasn't worried. Hell, the Sarge could probably disarm an ICBM in flight if he had to! "So it won't do more than annihilate Riverhead if it goes off, huh?"

The Sarge shook his head. "Not even that bad, is my guess. This building, for sure. The block, possibly. This thing is just a pony nuke."

A guess for Sarge was Gospel for Jimmy. "So what's our first move?"

"Well, that time-fuse says it's got almost two hours left. That should be plenty of time. I suppose we—" The Sarge broke off, stood as though listening to something. Jimmy smiled: The Sarge had done this several times before, with conventional but difficult bombs—explaining afterward that he was "trying to outthink the guy that built it"—so everything really was okay after all. Any minute now, the Sarge would—

—start running like a bastard, back the way they had come—

"Sarge!" Jimmy cried, but his instincts were good: he was already in motion. His legs were good too, and he had two of them: he was neck and neck with the Sarge within ten strides. Suddenly the Sarge put on the brakes and doubled back; Jimmy did not. As he cleared the door to the outside Jimmy could hear the Sarge's uneven footsteps coming up fast behind him again. Captain Whitfield and the other cops waiting outside scattered in all directions when they saw both running men.

The Sarge made a beeline for the Bomb Squad truck, leaped behind the wheel. He was carrying an airline bag.

"Sarge! Goddamn it—hey, *Sarge!*"

Sergeant Noah Gonzalez ignored him, started the truck and sped off.

Ralph spotted a likely-looking bitch, got close enough to smell her and growled deep in his throat. He had little difficulty in cutting her out of the pack she was with. He knew, as they did not, that in a matter of hours she would be panting for it. Confusing and mesmerizing her with his deep, softly accented voice, he led her away from her friends and into the darkness.

Sound Beach is a seasonally schizophrenic area of Long Island. For Ralph it was a walk on the wild side—literally. In the summer the vacation cottages are filled with the nearly-wealthy. In winter the region is sparsely populated by half-frozen college students from the nearby State University—and by packs of feral dogs. They are the watchdogs routinely abandoned by the nearly-wealthy at season's end. Dobermans, Shepherds. They pack-up, and raid garbage cans, and kill and eat the pets of the college students, and it is usually February or March before the county cops have shot the last of them. As a general rule, by the time they are hungry enough to attack a human, they are too weak to pull it off—though there are occasional exceptions.

Ralph Von Wau Wau neither smelled nor behaved domesticated, and he sounded like Arnold Schwarzenegger in pitch, tone, accent, and confidence; he could move among his savage cousins in relative safety. He had only been forced to fight twice in the five years he had been wintering on Long Island, and had won both fights handily. The feral dogs were cunning, but Ralph was intelligent, and it made all the difference.

Though he was a mutant, Ralph had all the normal urges of any red-blooded son of a bitch, and house pets just didn't do it for him. Too tame, too boring. His true preference was for women, and he was currently on intimate terms with half a dozen—but three were vacationing to the south with their husbands, two were preparing final exams for their students, and one was preparing to run for reelection. Ralph had not gotten laid in several weeks, and his opinion was that the next best thing to an adventurous and sophisticated lady was a wild outlaw bitch. They were less inventive, but more instinctively satisfying—and cross-fertile besides.

He had certain moral rules of his own devising, which might seem exotic to a human. He always fed a bitch, before and after. If necessary, he protected her to the best of his ability. If she got pregnant, he behaved as honorably as any other dog would—and scrutinized the offspring for indications that his mutation might have bred true—which so far it had not. If a hyperintelligent pup *had* resulted, he would have bent every effort to get it the same larynx-modification surgery he himself had once had, then taught it to talk. But by now he had almost given up hope.

He'd tried moving a few mates in with him, but it never worked out: they never really had enough in common to relate to one another, and it always upset them when he typed for hours at a time.

This particular bitch excited him a great deal, for reasons too subtle and subconscious for him to analyze. (Regrettably, the Freud of canine psychology has not yet emerged.) Something about the fur at the back of her neck, something about her walk, something about her smell . . . there was no defining it. She was new to him, puzzled by the contradiction between what her eyes and nose told her, and what her ears told her, and he found her innocence charming. She was cooperative, but not slavishly obedient. Her eyes flashed. Her scent was . . . piquant.

So they gave the rest of the pack the slip, and he took her to a warm and sheltered place he knew. There he opened a can of deviled ham—a rather extravagant wooing-gift, but one of the annoyingly few meats available in pop-top can format—and waited politely while she wolfed it down. Then they romped a bit, and nuzzled a bit, and presently he taught her some things about foreplay that astonished her. (The Masters & Johnson of canine physiology have yet to emerge as well—but when they do, Ralph Von Wau Wau will be massively represented in their footnotes.) Shortly after that, she taught him some things about hindplay. As mentioned, Ralph was a love 'em and leave 'em sort of fellow, but the summons from Jim and Paul MacDonald came at an extremely unfortunate, uh, juncture, and he was compelled to bring her halfway to Callahan's with him . . .

*   *   *

Joe and Susan Maser had sent their wife Susie on ahead to Callahan's because they wanted to put the finishing touches on the chili they intended to bring for the New Year's celebration; the summons came as Joe was stirring up the coals in the firebox of his woodstove. He dropped the poker and sprinted with Susan for the car, leaving the fire-door open on the stove. Pulling out of the driveway, he realized what would probably happen, but he didn't have time to do anything about it. Behind him, the draft whipped the fire to its hottest and sucked all the heat up the chimney . . . which had not been cleaned recently enough. Since Joe and Susan had also left the front door of the house open, much the same thing eventually happened to the building; by dawn all the Masers would own was the clothes on their backs and the contents of their pockets.

Similarly, Shorty Steinitz left his lovingly restored '57 Thunderbird jacked up with one wheel off by the side of Route 25A and ran the last quarter-mile; he never saw it again. Lady Sally McGee was entertaining a very old and dear friend when the call came; he had never been intended to remain in that position for more than fifteen minutes, but the silken cords were strong, and he could not reach the slipknots. Pyotr left his bottle of breakfast sitting on his kitchen table, and few foods go bad faster or uglier than blood. And Bill Gerrity was caught in the middle of getting dressed: this would have been embarrassing for anyone, but for Bill "half-dressed" for a party meant dark nylons, purple garter belt, black panties and an hour's worth of makeup (high heels, too, but he ditched them within the first half block); in the three and a half miles he had to jog to Callahan's, he was forced to hospitalize four young toughs who mistook him for a homosexual, two policemen who correctly identified him as an attractive nuisance, and a persistent politician who simply would not get out of the way.

It was not, in short, without cost that the men and women of Callahan's Place answered the Call, even though nearly all of them were getting ready to go there at the time. But it is a matter of proud record that every single one of them paid the cost, unhesitatingly. Within an hour, the Place was packed to capacity with all the regulars past and present, with all the people to whom this tavern had ever been *home* for a time, and nobody had any complaints to make. The MacDonald Brothers had followed up their initial Call with a synopsis of the situation; everyone arrived with a fair grasp of what was going on.

Josie Bauer was the first to arrive, of course, since it took her literally no time at all; she materialized before the bar, took the shot glass of Irish whiskey that Callahan was holding out for her and set it down on the bartop, plucked the cigar from his lips and kissed him firmly. "You sneaky bastard," she murmured. "I never guessed. I should have guessed. You must be from *much* further up the line than my outfit."

"Not as much as you might think, hon'," he told her.

She turned to Mary and kissed her, too. "Hang in there, sugar. He'll be okay."

The next arrival was Shorty, and he did just what Josie had done. I'd be willing to bet Shorty had never kissed another male in his life before, but he did so with no hesitation or sign of embarrassment. That set the pattern. Every new arrival, and those already present, collected a shot and a kiss from Callahan and his daughter. No one drank; we waited for Mike to propose the toast. All of us were smiling, and all of us were crying, and all of us were touching, and none of us said a word, save for occasional briefly murmured greetings to old friends too seldom seen. No one had anything pertinent to say, and no one felt the need to mouth off without saying anything; it was enough to be together, to share whatever would come. I saw friends I hadn't seen in years—Ben, Stan, Don, Mary and Stephen, both Jims, Big Tom, Susan, Betsy, Mark, Chris, Robert and Ginny, Herb and Ricia, Diana, Joe and Gay, Jack, Vinny, Railroad George, Ted, Gordy, Dee for Chrissakes, Tony and Susan, Wendy, Bob, Kirby, Eleanor, Charlie and Evelyn, and of course David— and it came to me as the crowd grew and the Place filled up that I could not have asked for a better time or place to die. There was noplace on Earth or off it that I loved as much, nor any people I had ever loved better—no, not even the wife and daughter I'd killed a decade ago by doing my own brake-job with a self-help book—and New Year's Eve seemed an appropriately backassward date for Judgment Day.

After a little more than a half hour of murmured greetings, multiple embraces and general warm happiness, Paul MacDonald spoke to Callahan. "Okay, Mike. Everybody who's going to arrive in time is here now."

The room became totally quiet, filled with a mood of exuberant desperation. The locker room before the big game. Backstage waiting for the house lights to go down. The hold of the Huey as the LZ appears in the distance.

We were as ready as we were going to be.

Callahan nodded slowly. "It's about time," he rumbled. He trod his cigar underfoot and lit a new one. "It's all about time." He poured a shot of Bushmill's for himself, walked slowly around the bar. "Isn't it?" The sawdust squealed under his boots. Fast Eddie left the piano and tossed a couple of sticks of dry birch onto the fire; there was a crackle as the bark began to catch, and that fine sharp-sweet smell of burning birch joined the symphony of pleasant smells in the room. Callahan toed the chalk line, faced the rattling hearth. I didn't mind the tears; they fell too quickly to obscure my vision. He raised his glass, and we all raised ours. The bright lights shattered on all that glass and the room sparkled like a vast crystal.

"To the human race," Mike Callahan said clearly in that gravelly baritone. "God help us, every one." He drank off the Bushmill's in one long, slow draught, smacked his lips and whipped the glass underhand into the fireplace.

"**To the human race**," we chorused, and the largest barrage of glasses in the history of Callahan's Place began.

And when the great shout and cheer had subsided and the last shard of glass skittered to its final resting place, we began to build something.

* * *

I perceived it in musical terms, of course: to me what we built was something like a vast symphony orchestra, save that in addition to the usual ordnance of a full orchestra it incorporated saxophones, electric guitars, tin flutes, tablas, trap drums, Yamaha synthesizers, steel drums, vocoders, kazoos, baby rattles, Zal Yanovsky's Electric Gorgle and the Big Jukebox in *Close Encounters,* included every means the race has ever devised for making music and some that haven't been invented yet, the whole thing integrated into a vast tapestry of sonic and tonal textures that was indescribable and probably unimaginable—certainly I had never imagined anything like it before that night—and primevally satisfying to what a Buddhist might call my "third ear."

Imagine that you assembled such a superorchestra in a room. First there is cacophony, as each musician sounds his or her instrument and limbers it up, no individual or group predominating for more than a few seconds. Then one loud true voice takes up and holds a 440 cps A, and gradually everyone tunes to it; for several seconds everyone is playing the same note and it's like a giant "OM" chant. Then it diverges again, as each player goes into scales or warmup exercises. Imagine then that, seemingly by pure random chance, the vast assemblage of instruments happens to stumble onto a single, stupendous chord, an accidental aural architecture of terrifying beauty, a chord so complex that the most knowledgable musician there cannot name it, yet so *elemental* that each feels he has always known it in his heart. It holds, swells, falters momentarily as percussive notes fade and lungs empty of breath and bows reach the limit of their traverse, then returns and steadies and fills the room to bursting, each musician thinking, *keep playing— yes, try to notice and remember what note you're playing, but for God's sake* **keep playing,** *if we lose this thing we may never find it again and if that happens I believe I may need to die—*

The thing we built was like that. There was no sound to it, any more than there was substance to it, but it hung invisibly in the air around us, annihilating the space between us, and to me that's music. The 440 A that we all tuned to was the voice, the essence, the nature of Mike Callahan, echoed and amplified by the MacDonalds. But neither he nor they led us to that "chord"—we found that ourselves. Shortly it changed from something as static as the word "chord" implies to something dynamic, as though individual musicians, confident now that the chord would not be lost, began to jam around it, to dress it with trills and arpeggios and scraps of melody and rhythmic accents; it changed from a pretty sound to true music, although no human ear could have resolved music like that. It was timeless, like raga, and frantic, like bebop; it swung like Carl Perkins, and it purred like Betty Carter; it was simple like Bach and complex like Ray Charles; it was hot and cool and hip and square and lush and spare—I know no music can be all those things together, but this was. In the back of my mind I could hear Lord Buckley, rest his ticker, talkin' 'bout, "My lords and my ladies, I'm gon' hip you: you may have heard a lot of jam sessions blowin' off, you may o' heard o' New Orleans flips, you may have heard it Chicago style, you may have heard all kinds o' jazz jumpin' the wildest an' the most insane, you may have heard o' many musical insane flips, but you studs an' stallions an' cats an' kitties *never dug any session like these cats BLEW!...*"

To others present it did not suggest music at all. Shorty Steinitz was a sculptor; to him it was as though all of us struck together simultaneously at a magnificent block of Carrera marble, reducing it in an instant to a perfect and complete statue, which began in that moment of its creation to walk and talk. Susie Maser was a Modern dance choreographer; she felt that we were inventing zero-gravity dance together. Indeed, Long-Drink McGonnigle, who had cherished a perverse interest in entomology ever since February 7, 1964, felt that whatever it was resembled pictures he'd seen of webs woven by spiders in free fall, in Skylab. Doc Webster saw us all as neurons learning to work together, to form "... well, not a brain, not even a small one—but a ganglion, by God!" Tom Hauptmann, the former minister, perceived what we built as a perfect prayer, pleasing to God, who is a tough critic of prayers.

I do not know all this from having compared notes afterward. I knew it then, and everyone there knew and understood the analogy-mode that worked for me just as well as I knew theirs. Just because I perceived it as music didn't make it music for Fast Eddie: the little piano man felt that we were setting up and executing a hundred-cushion billiard shot in ultraslow motion and cascading instant-replay. Of course, he appreciated my appreciation of it as music—but no more than did Tom Hauptmann, who is totally tone deaf (or rather, had been until then). Perhaps the most insightful analogy we conceived was that of Joe and Susan and Susie Maser, who saw us all as building a group marriage akin to their own triad.

Or perhaps it came from Noah Gonzalez, who pictured us constructing, entirely by intuition, a cobalt bomb.

All this happened at the top of our minds, in the forefront of our combined consciousness. Along with that, we were simultaneously, but not separately, growing closer to one another, getting to know each other in even greater depth than we already did, sharing and cherishing. Tom, for instance, was discovering music for the first time in his life, and finding it both more and less than he had imagined it must be. Long-Drink and the Doc and I were discerning some interesting things at the root of our long-standing rivalry at punning. Tommy Janssen was understanding for the first time why heterosexual Bill Gerrity enjoyed wearing drag. Tom Hauptmann was learning things about eroticism from Josie Bauer that would have shocked him cockeyed an hour before, and she was learning equally unsettling things about chastity from him. All of us were learning things from the Callahans, husband, wife and daughter, that I can't put down here. It's not that you don't have the words. You don't have the concepts to put words on.

At Callahan's Place we were used to sharing, to letting down barriers, to opening up to and for one another. Callahan's frequently proclaimed policy of violently discouraging snoopy questions had always been a sham, a custom honored more in the breach than in the observance, a prohibition which we now perceived was designed to teach us to learn how to circumvent it—hell, the Cheerful Charlies had it down pat. Not to mention the MacDonalds. Or Callahan himself, who sucked secrets out of you with his twinkling eyes. We thought that we already knew what it meant to *be one* together; we had been students of sharing here for many years together.

This was more, deeper, stronger, better. A sizable fraction of the people there were folks I didn't know well or at all, ex-regulars from before my time who had still been alive and around to hear The Call, and Walter the failed suicide: while devoting the bulk of our individual and collective attention to the thing that we were building, we became blood brothers and sisters without wasting time or words.

Words. It is interesting that none of us perceived the thing we built in terms of a structure of words. It was sheer pattern-recognition—images, gestalts, sensory impressions and emotional rhythms, a nonstop cascade of data that reached even the subvocalized level only in scattered, fragmentary form, like verbal buckshot:

(warm!/and so when she died I/Heavenly Father . . . / merry, by God!/roll 'em baby/ you're beautiful/thank you/ you're beautiful too/thank you/It's beautiful/always wanted to tell you that I/do that again/ain't it?/never thought it could be like/pulsing/steady now/ere do I remember this fr/ fast!/would have done the same thing my/take it/strong!/ remember re-member reMember ream ember/more treble, we're losing the highs/hi!/hie/hai!/never lose the/high/I/eye/ aye! /LOVE/U/ ewe/ hue/ yew /YOU/ too /U2/ to / two / whoo!/ who?/hew/Hugh/yoo hoo!/YOU!)

It went on forever, for whole seconds, repeating and changing and building like a series of choruses in jazz without any of us ever forming a coherent sentence in words. And yet when the time came to speak, we found that we could—although we were one, we retained our individual voices and the personalities they represented.

No, put quotes around "speak" and "voices." If there'd been a stranger in the room, he would not have heard or seen or felt a thing. To him we would have been a roomful of strange and twisted people, standing around a snoring basketball player, smiling dementedly at nothing at all, in silence . . .

"All right, ladies and gents," Callahan said, his voice clear and strong in my skull, "Let's get this show on the road. We need a plan. The floor is open."

"There ain't but the one plan," I said. "We get the Roaches on the phone and invite 'em over for a beer."

"Here?" two or three minds yelped.

"Sure. We badly lack data, and short of waking up Finn the only source is the Cockroaches themselves."

(A funny little thing happened then, entirely below the surface, that was over in an instant. I'm rather ashamed of it—but it's illustrative of something that was happening all around the room, so I'll tell it. A primitive ape who clings to my brainstorm still wanted Mary Callahan, still perceived Finn as a rival—worse, a successful rival—worst, a superior rival. That ape heard me calmly trying to cope with a problem that had Finn catatonic with fear . . . and smiled, displaying the kind of teeth that apes only have on Frazetta covers for Tarzan books. For an instant, it felt smug—*I* felt smug. For a picosecond or two, the ape fantasized outcomes in which all of us survived except Finn, in which—just for once, oh, Lord!—I ended up with the girl I wanted.

And then I saw Mary looking at Finn, and I beat that ape to death with a club. Maybe Finn was paralyzed by fear, not because he was more of a coward than I, but because he knew more about the situation. Or faced more stringent penalties than I did. My smugness rested on ego, my courage on ignorance.

Why I mention it is this: There were no unburied hatchets in Callahan's Bar—there never had been for very long. But now even the buried hatchets were starting to decompose underground, to rust away to nothing. I would always want Mary—but the best I could ever hope for would be to help her get what *she* wanted. I guess I was learning to live with that. Similar mini-epiphanies were happening all around the room.)

"But why should they give us *any* data?" Mary asked. "What's our leverage?"

"We've got data *they* want."

"We do?"

"Locked up between Finn's ears, I'm sure of it. I don't know what it is he knows; apparently he doesn't know either. But the bugs came one Jesus long way to learn it. They're a cowardly race; they don't go in person to any place that a scout has failed to report back from without some powerful motivation; that's why Finn is so baffled. Well, they can't be that curious about *us* because they don't know us from pond scum, so it *has* to be Finn. Something in his memory tapes is worth the risk. Maybe we can cut a deal."

"I wouldn't bet on it," the Drink said.

"McGonnigle, you are going to have to. Right now."

"Jake's right," Callahan said. "Unless anybody here knows how to disable a bunch of invisible satellites and convince NORAD to go to DEFCON ONE within the next half hour, we haven't got much choice." He frowned. A telepathic frown itches. "Another thing. We have to call the Cockroaches *right away,* and get them to come directly here from Mars, as quietly as possible. If they just come look over the whole planet, NORAD *is* going to spot them—and find out that its ABMs don't work anymore."

"So what?" several people asked.

"Suppose we resolve this Cockroach situation somehow—but meanwhile the Joint Chiefs find out that all their warheads are worthless. So do the Soviets. Unstable situation. And it leaves the USSR dominating Europe. Finn was right: his scheme only works if the players don't know about it. It's too late to undo the scheme, so we've got to go with it. That means the defense of Earth has to be handled in this room."

That brought a buzz of voices so sharp that it spilled over into the thing that we were building with the other ninety percent of our minds, sending a small ripple of discord through the sonic tapestry, as though there was a printer's error in the sheet music. And then was felt the presence of Lady Sally McGee, a warm, competent, reassuringly strong and calm voice in our heads.

"Lighten up, darlings! This is a party—we're here to usher in the new year! It turns out we'll have to actually *do* something to accomplish that for a change, but there's no reason we can't enjoy ourselves, is there? This could be fun! Now, I think it would be a good idea if all those without concrete useful suggestions were to shut the hell up."

Fast Eddie spoke up in the silence. "De foist t'ing we gotta do is hide Finn."

Even Callahan blinked. "Hide Finn?"

"He's de only card we got—so we slip it up our sleeve. Den we dummy up."

In my head I saw (and therefore everybody saw) a little cartoon, with word balloons and borders and crosshatching and everything, in which a comic caricature of a cockroach in a pressure suit spoke to Callahan: *"Where is Txffu Mpwfs?"* "Never heard of him." *"An extremely powerful and dangerous scout; he would have fought valiantly."* "Sorry, haven't seen him." *"Then how is it that you seem to know who I am?"* "Oh, I've made a study of lower life forms—"

It did seem like a gambit with some distinct possibilities.

"Eddie, you're a genius," I said. "There's one hitch. Jim, Paul—can you lie telepathically?"

They looked troubled. "We could lie to you; we've got years more experience. To a mind as trained and experienced as ours—possibly. It would be like playing forty-two chess games at once: there's so much to *keep track of* in a telepathic lie. To an alien critter that's never touched a human mind before—," their eyes met briefly, "—no sweat."

"Maybe," Tommy Janssen said, "we should tell the Roaches we spotted Finn before he got near us, and annihilated him—make us look more powerful, like."

Callahan shook his head. "Just wrong, son. That would make us the equals of a Cockroach. We're *superior*—we never even *noticed* Finn. Some little automatic system swept him up and we paid no mind, interstellar invasion didn't even make the papers." He grinned. "Yeah, I think maybe we could pull this off—for a few minutes, anyway. We might just put them enough off-balance to find out what we need to know."

Doc Webster spoke for all of us. "You're our spokesman, Mike."

He kept grinning and quoted Lord Buckley again. "'Well if I ain't, I'm a great big fat groovy pole on a rough hill on the way there.' Okay, while I'm planning the con, you boys hide Fipp somewheres."

Gee, that sounds easy, doesn't it? I mean, compared to trying to map out a strategy for outsmarting alien monsters, hiding a guy doesn't sound like a big deal.

A guy who stands damn near seven feet tall and weighs about the same as a Harley-Davidson...

The best thought we had was to lay him down on the floor behind the bar, but the Cockroaches might very well burn their way in from above—and besides, Finn *snored*. In three stages.

Then I happened to think of what Finn's physique had always reminded me of. It was a chilly January night; we had plenty of coats. What cinched it was that his shirt had two breast pockets that snapped closed: coats hung from that low reached to the floor. When we were done, you could hardly hear the muffled snore; it sounded like a failing fridge compressor somewhere in the next room.

"How do we know the Roaches will hear a telepathic call?" Doc Webster asked worriedly.

"They will," Jim and Paul assured him. "They're not telepaths any more than you folks are, but they'll hear just as you did. We got their 'address-code' from Finn before he went bye-bye."

"Are you sure you can reach them? Last I heard your range was still pretty limited—"

"That was years ago, Doc. And this time we have twice as many minds around to help drive the signal. We're within ... uh ... Roach's Limit."

The Doc glared at them. "Obviously you don't understand the gravity of the situation."

Telepathy has its drawbacks. Ordinarily most of us would have missed puns that esoteric.

"All right," Mary said, "by now they've finished checking out Mars and they're shaping orbit for Earth. How do we do this?"

"It breaks down into three parts," her father told her. "Message, target location, and delivery. Me and Jim/Paul'll do the talking. Mary, you and Josie and Joe and Ben and Stan savvy planetary ballistics: you folks aim the beam—you're in charge, darlin', you're the only one of us that's actually been off Earth. Jake, you and the rest of the gang push the message where it's pointed—the way we did back when we first met Jim, get it? Any questions?"

There were none.

"Okay, let's do it."

Our music grew, built, swelled, gathered energy from nameless places and expanded in all directions, churned itself to a mighty crescendo, began to throb and pulse and crackle with contained power. As it did so, vision faded. Reality faded. Physically impossible though it was, suddenly we were all *touching* each other at the same time. I had been to an orgy once, and found it disappointing; this was what I had wanted it to be. It felt like what the Sixties had tried, and failed, to be. Like my childhood conception of the Catholic Heaven. Like making love with God.

The last time I'd been on this plane, helping Jim MacDonald to find and reach his lost, tormented, terrified brother Paul, it had been pleasurable, but not nearly this ecstatic. On that occasion, we had all perceived ourselves as standing behind an imaginary truck, stuck in an imaginary ditch, and had put our shoulders and backs into helping get it unstuck. There was no truck now, and whatever was in its place was not stuck—but in some fashion we *strained* now as we had strained then, put all our strength behind a massive, convulsive common effort.

We tried to hide that. Have you ever lifted a very heavy object in front of a stranger you wanted to impress, and tried not merely to lift the crushing weight, but to make it look easy? In just that fashion, we drew figurative breath, fashioned a mighty Shout—and then tried to couch it in quiet, conversational tones, as though we could shout much louder than that if we wanted to.

This time period (*) is a second, we bellowed calmly. **You have thirty of them in which to bargain for your life.**

In the instant that contact was established, we knew just how flimsy our bluff was.

There was only one Master. We didn't even know then just what a break that was. The telepathic aspect of the creature was largely untranslatable, but you might think of it manifesting as a kind of giant space-going shark, a moving appetite, a vast, fast, terrible eating-machine which saw its purpose to be turning everything edible in the universe into shark shit. Like a shark it was implacable, remorseless, unreachable. What made it much more terrible than any shark was that it was highly intelligent and very learned.

This doesn't begin to convey it. The thing was *alien,* and nothing on Terra is as old or cold or deadly as it was. If I'd been alone, I think I'd have snapped like a twig and begged it to kill me quickly. But Mike Callahan was with me, legs planted wide, thumbs hooked over his apron, jaw outthrust challengingly . . . I could see him through my eyelids . . .

It must have known telepathic races in the past; mental contact did not startle it. Its answering "voice" was no "louder" than ours, but it really *was* sending at the low end of its strength—it was much more powerful than we combined were. But it didn't know that—we bluffed it!

"WHO ARE YOU THAT A MASTER SHOULD BARGAIN WITH YOU FOR ITS LIFE?"

"—**twenty-nine**—" Callahan said for all of us.

"STATE YOUR ASKING PRICE."

"**One: full and candid disclosure of your purpose and intentions here. Two: your promise not to disturb any sentient in this system. Three: your immediate departure. Four: your promise never to return unsummoned.**"

None of this was in English. That is, it left Callahan's mind as English but passed through the minds of Jim and Paul, who knew as much of the Masters' language as Finn did, and by hearing it through their "ears," we understood it independent of any grammar or vocabulary. The English of it doesn't begin to convey the monstrous arrogance of the bluff Mike was running.

"NO MASTER HAS *EVER* BEEN 'SUMMONED.' I GO WHERE I LIST, AND DISTURB ALL WHO PERCEIVE ME. WHAT—"

"**Countdown resumes. Twenty-eight**—," Mike interrupted—and a telepathic interruption is ruder than any other kind, I think.

I tried to imagine the situation from the creature's perspective. Humans were sufficiently advanced as a race to be able to hang out a telepathic No Trespassing sign for it, seemed completely unawed by its own majestic power—yet they restricted themselves to a single planet, of a single star system, and the only technology visible thereon seemed primitive. They were either suicidally brave—or they had something up their sleeves. The Masters were, as Finn had told us, remorselessly logical: its safest move was to play along until such time as it determined positively that we were bluffing, and *then* implode our planet, leaving no witnesses to its humiliation.

But it *hated* acknowledging any non-Master life form as an equal, even as a bargaining ploy. Mike got all the way down to twenty-five—and my heart got about three-quarters of the way up my esophagus—when it said:

"IT SUITS ME TO DIVULGE MY PURPOSE HERE. SUBSEQUENTLY, WE MAY DETERMINE TOGETHER WHETHER ITS FULFILLMENT WILL DISTURB LOCAL SENTIENTS, AND THE PROBABLE TIME OF MY DEPARTURE."

"Speak. And make it snappy."

"I SEEK A MISSING SLAVE. SENT TO SCOUT THIS SYSTEM, IT FAILED TO REPORT BACK. I SEEK IT, OR ITS REMAINS. ONCE I HAVE IT, I HAVE NO FURTHER INTEREST IN REMAINING OR RETURNING HERE."

"Goodbye, then. Neither your slave nor its remains are here."

You might reasonably translate the Master's reply as **"SHARKSHIT."** It had raised its "voice" slightly: it was getting angry.

We kept our tone level. **"—Twenty-four—"**

When I was a kid in school, I always sat in the back of the classroom. If things got too boring, I'd do a Slow Fade. You move your desk back and to the right imperceptibly slowly, about six inches per minute, toward the back door and out into the hall. If you do it slowly enough, the teacher never notices you leave. In a similar manner, Paul Mac-Donald began now to withdraw from the thing we had all built in Callahan's Place, without advertising his departure. It helped that his brother's telepathic aspect was so nearly identical to his own. I don't think anyone else noticed— maybe they never played Slow Fade—and I kept my own realization from the common awareness, did my best not to think about it even to myself. While we were talking to the front of the alien's mind, Paul was sneaking around the back . . .

"THE SLAVE WAS WELL-DEFENDED," it was saying. **"I CAN BELIEVE YOU OVERCAME IT; BUT IF SO IT WOULD HAVE BEEN A MEMORABLE EVENT."**

"Perhaps for one such as you," Callahan agreed. **"Our automatic defenses are capable, and do not require our attention."**

"THEN WHY ARE YOU SPEAKING TO *ME*?"

"Amused curiosity. Your mind is singularly ugly."

Oddly, it did not take offense. Every entity it had ever met in its centuries of existence had feared it; it did not know how to react to a direct insult. But it *did* get angrier— because we were wasting its time. **"EVEN IF YOU HAD**

ANNIHILATED THE SLAVE, THERE WOULD HAVE BEEN A
COMPONENT LEFT, INDESTRUCTIBLE BY ANY KNOWN
FORCE. IT WOULD HAVE BEEN LOCATED HERE—" It sent
a sort of three-dimensional X-ray picture of Finn's head,
and clearly visible beneath and behind his right ear, between
skull and brain, was a little nodule that looked like a marble.
"IT IS A DATAFILE CONTAINING EVERYTHING PERCEIVED
BY THE SLAVE SINCE ITS LAST MILKING. I REQUIRE IT
IMMEDIATELY."

"You grow boring," Callahan said. "Countdown resumes—"

"I WILL TEAR APART YOUR STAR!"

Callahan made no reply. He made a throat-cutting gesture
to us, and we broke the connection.

There was no chatter. Less than half a minute on the
countdown, on our bluff.

"What did you get, Paul?" Callahan snapped, and I became aware for the first time that Paul MacDonald was back
among us telepathically as well as physically. He tended to
"blend in" with Jim's aspect, like an echo, which why
it had been possible for him to get away with a Slow Fade.

He made a convulsive mental effort, and did something
like a file memory dump, sending information in a block
rather than bit by bit, to all of us at once. In a matter of a
second, we knew everything he had learned. Grasping it
took me a few seconds more.

I have to put it in figurative terms. A lot of this stuff
doesn't go into words; worse, the memories turn insub-
stantial as I try to translate them. Paul had sneaked in an
unguarded back window of the creature's mind, while we
occupied it at the front door. He had strolled around in some
of the mustier back files of an immense storehouse of memories for a matter of whole seconds, teaching himself how
to understand the operating language, the file-finder system,
the retrieval commands—reconnoitering while keeping a
low profile. He didn't get all he'd hoped for, he ran out of
seconds, but Paul was a seasoned professional at tiptoeing

through human minds, and he came away with more from this alien mind than I would have believed possible.

The majority of what he learned was incomprehensible or irrelevant or otherwise useless. The creature's name, to pick a basic example, was utterly untranslatable. We could no longer think of it as a Cockroach, and like Mary we refused to call it a Master. We reached an instant group consensus on what to call it: The Beast. (And hoped that we had its number.)

The Beast was a pervert. Don't ask me to describe what kind of pervert it was, or what constituted "normal" for its race. I don't want to think about either one. Please just take my word for it that it was, by its own lights, disgusting. It was *not* ashamed of itself. Shame is a kind of self-hatred, and no Master is capable of hating—or loving—itself. But it did wish strongly that it could be other than it was, and that is as close as such a being can come to shame. (Not close enough, in my opinion.)

Its perversion had recently become known to its kind. Social faux pas on a cosmic scale: it was now and forever an outcast, a renegade, to be slain on sight. Its slaves had been reprogrammed to others. It was alone. To one of its race this fate was simply intolerable. Masters cannot live in Coventry. This is weird, since they are not a gregarious race under the best of circumstances. They don't need each other's *attention,* the way humans do, but they positively require each other's *respect.* The Beast had exactly two psychologically feasible alternatives; to suicide, or declare war on its entire race.

In the billion or so years of Master-recorded history, only a very few of the very few outcasts had ever chosen the latter alternative, and their names were metaphoric symbols for evil itself. But The Beast was a *real* pervert.

It was also a logical pervert. No force or combination of forces it knew could seriously threaten its race. But it wasn't (The Beast was prepared, being a pervert, to admit to itself) strictly true that *everything* was known to the Masters. For instance, once in a very long time (even by Master standards), a scout slave failed to report back. Scouts were so heavily armed and defended that it was difficult to imagine anything capable of destroying one before it could get off a report. (No Master in the Universe was permitted to be as heavily armed as a typical scout, since a Master, unlike a slave, could bring himself to turn a weapon on another Master. I know that doesn't make sense in human terms. Very little about the Masters does.) An AWOL scout meant either that someone had destroyed it, someone who could perhaps be used, or that the scout had—incredibly—mal-functioned in some way, in which case its own weaponry might be salvageable.

The risk was horrible. A Master is not defended as well as a scout either.

It was a mad gamble, and The Beast knew it, but it was a pervert and doomed. Desperate and raging, it had followed the trail of Txffu Mpwfs across the big empty spaces to the place where he was known as Mickey Finn, hoping to find some terrorweapon it could use to avenge itself, and found . . . a bunch of barflies, a few time traveling Micks, two telepathic psychiatrists and a talking dog. Callahan's Bar on New Year's Eve.

"All right," Callahan said in our heads as we finished assimilating the burst of largely useless data that included this, "we've got it right where we want it. At T minus ten seconds, we tell it we've changed our minds: we're not going to kill it after all. It's too disgusting to kill. We're going to ignore it—and call the other Masters and demand that they come remove their garbage from our system at once. That should—"

He screamed then, with his mind and with his throat. I don't suppose I'd ever thought to hear Mike Callahan scream. I didn't hear the physical scream, of course, because sounds drown each other out and I and everyone else in the room were screaming, too, but mental screams *don't* drown each other out, each one registered with individual clarity. Amazing that I had time to register such trivia, with The Beast loose in my brain . . .

* * *

"ENTROPY!"

The beast was very angry; that was the strongest curse it knew.

"JUST AS I FEARED! IT WAS NOT A WEAPON WHICH DISABLED TXFFU MPWFS, BUT A DISEASE. THAT 'LOVE' FUNGUS. USELESS TO ME!"

Paul hadn't been as careful as he thought. We should have remembered: Finn thought faster than a human being; so would his Masters. Probably they thought even faster than him.

In the instant of opening communication we had told The Beast the rate at which we processed information—by establishing a second as a significant interval for us—and it had been outthinking us ever since. It had had plenty of time to spot Paul stumbling around in the back of its brain, without alerting him. It had learned a great deal about telepathy from him, and then had hidden in his pocket, as it were, and been brought back home by him. His data-broadcast had opened us all up, allowed The Beast to access our files and study *us*. Our cover was blown sky-high. Jim and Paul MacDonald were effectively dead, their minds torn out, their personalities annihilated, their bodies and brains kept alive to serve The Beast as a telepathic transceiver.

I was caught. Swallowed by The Beast. Damn it, it was *just* like being swallowed by a Beast, the size of the one that got Pinocchio. My surroundings went away, my telepathic companions went away, my eyes and my mind found black nothingness in all directions—I tried to cast around with my arms and discovered that I could not find my body anymore. The audible screams, including my own, were now inaudible; so were the mental ones. There was just the Master and me. All my strings were cut.

"OR PERHAPS NOT *ENTIRELY* USELESS AFTER ALL," it went on thoughtfully. "I SEE POSSIBILITIES . . ."

I snapped, shrieked at him: *"Motherfucker!"* It seemed to echo.

"IT IS A MINOR COMPONENT OF MY PERVERSION THAT
I AM NOT. YOU OUGHT TO TRY TO ENJOY YOUR CON-
SCIOUSNESS. THE ONE YOU CALL FINN WILL WAKE, AND
THEN I WILL OWN IT AGAIN, AND THEN YOUR CON-
SCIOUSNESS WILL CEASE. SOON, AS YOU RECKON TIME:
YOU HAVE NO TIME TO WASTE."

"When Mick wakes up you're gonna be the first Shark
that ever got killed by his own Finn!" I only half-believed
it, but I badly needed that half. My sanity hung from it.

"I CONCEDE THAT IT HAS DISOBEYED PROGRAMMING
AN UNPRECEDENTED NUMBER OF TIMES — ONCE, FOR AN
INTERVAL MEASURABLE IN YOUR GREAT LONG SEC-
ONDS." Dimly I knew somehow that the Beast was not
talking only to me, but talking privately to each of us, by
time-sharing at a horrendous rate, the way a TV tube redraws
each line of pixels so quickly that you never see them dis-
appear. "IT WILL NOT DO SO AGAIN."

"Finn loves us!" I cried, while thinking, *Finn loves* one
of us. "Even if he didn't, he'd fight you—because you're
evil!"

"HOW AM I EVIL?"

"You're a murderer!"

"INCORRECT. I HAVE NEVER KILLED ANY SENTIENT
ENTITY."

"You and your kind killed Finn's entire race!"

"INCORRECT. WE HAVE NEVER KILLED ANY RACE."

"Fuck you. Mick told us the truth."

"CORRECT. YOU MISUNDERSTOOD IT. ITS RACE IS NOT
DEAD, MERELY IN STORAGE. IT TOLD YOU THAT EACH
OF ITS PEOPLE HAS BEEN RECORDED ON A MOLECULE OF
ITS OWN, DOWN TO THE LAST MEMORY. ALL WE KILLED
WERE CELLS, AS YOU DO WHEN YOU PARE YOUR OWN
FINGERNAILS. THE ESSENCE OF FINN'S PEOPLE, THEIR
CONSCIOUSNESS AND MEMORIES AND GENETIC PATTERNS,
ARE NOT ENDED. THEY COULD BE RECREATED AT ANY
INSTANT, A TRIVIAL MATTER OF SYNTHESIZING ENOUGH
PROTEIN. THEY ARE NOT DEAD, MERELY DISPLACED IN
TIME. LIKE MICHAEL CALLAHAN."

Oof.

"IT IS A SHAME THAT THE METHOD HE USES TO TRAVEL IN TIME IS UNSUITABLE FOR MASTERS—THAT WOULD BE A MIGHTY WEAPON INDEED. I MUST GIVE THOUGHT TO ADAPTING IT—"

"You're worse than a murderer," I yelled. "You're a *slaver,* and an arrogant pervert!" Dimly it occurred to me that a videotape recording of the interior of Callahan's Place at this moment must look pretty strange: a roomful of people apparently hollering abuse at each other. Or was I actually yelling, with my throat? I tried to figure out how to regain control of my senses, groping around in the dark for the controls.

"DOES YOUR RACE NOT ENSLAVE CHIMPANZEES AND DOLPHINS, THOUGH THEY ARE CLEARLY SENTIENT? AND WORSE, DO NOT MEMBERS OF YOUR SPECIES ROUTINELY ENSLAVE *EACH OTHER?* THIS IS PERVERTED ENOUGH TO REVOLT EVEN ME: IN ALL OF TIME, NO MASTER HAS EVER DONE SUCH A THING."

Damn him, he was getting to me, he kept poking little holes in all my postulates, undermining my moral position and turning my righteous anger into nothing more than the helpless rage of the victim. I tried to ignore him as I struggled to invest my body again.

"CAN YOU, INCIPIENT ALCOHOLIC WHO ARE AT-TRACTED ONLY TO FAT WOMEN AND ARE COMFORTABLE ONLY HERE IN THIS ROOM WITH PSYCHOLOGICAL CRIP-PLES LIKE YOURSELF, CALL ME A PERVERT? AS FOR AR-ROGANCE, CAN YOU, WHO KILLED YOUR FAMILY TO SAVE A FEW DOLLARS AND SHOW OFF IMAGINARY MECHANICAL COMPETENCE, CALL ME ARROGANT?"

My universe of blackness began spinning around me. Don't ask me how blackness can spin. I had to make it stop or I would go yammering insane, and the only way to do that was to get my eyes open. Damn it, I had lived in this goddam skull all my life, navigated my way around it blind drunk, done a cold-restart of all systems after thousands of interludes of natural or unnatural unconsciousness—why the hell couldn't I tell where anything *was?*

Let's see. The ears should be the simplest; fewer bits of data to integrate than eyes. First get hearing back, then go for the big stuff. Sound off, ears, I can't see you.

"I HAVE NEARLY REACHED YOU NOW. SOON I WILL BE PHYSICALLY PRESENT, AND ABLE TO RESTART THE SLAVE FINN."

"He'll find a way to beat you. He won't let his wife down!"

There was a sort of far-off rumbling. Miles away up its alimentary canal, The Beast was grinning. "I WILL PROMISE HIM THAT IF HE HELPS ME TO . . . *RECORD* YOU ALL, AND FIGHTS MY WAR FOR ME, I WILL REVIVE HIS PEOPLE, AND GIVE THEM A PLANET TO USE AS THEY WISH. THIS ONE WILL DO ADMIRABLY. HE WILL COOPERATE."

No, damn it, it was *not* a faraway, metaphorical rumbling. It was close by, and real. My hearing was coming back—

—and The Beast was burning his way through the roof of Callahan's Place.

"I WILL GIVE YOU A RIDDLE," it went on conversationally. "THERE IS A RACE OF CREATURES ON THIS PLANET WHICH IS CLOSELY RELATED TO MY OWN, THOUGH MUCH DEGENERATED FROM THE PURE STOCK. A SMALL GROUP OF THESE CREATURES COULD EASILY KILL ONE OF YOU, YET NONE HAVE EVER DONE SO: THEIR WORST 'CRIME' IS THAT, LIKE EVERYTHING ELSE IN YOUR ECOSYSTEM, THEY COMPETE WITH YOU FOR FOOD—AND LOSE IN THE COMPETITION, EVERY TIME. THESE CREATURES ARE CLEARLY AND UNMISTAKABLY SENTIENT. YET YOU SLAUGHTER THEM EVERY TIME YOU ENCOUNTER THEM, BY THE VILEST MEANS KNOWN TO YOU. CAN YOU NAME THESE ENTITIES? AND CAN YOU, IN LIGHT OF THIS INFORMATION, STILL CONSIDER *ME* EVIL?"

I heard scattered crashes, felt distant pain, understood that one of my friends had been hurt by a falling piece of burning ceiling.

"I AM HERE," The Beast said. "AH—YOU ARE EVEN UGLIER IN PERSON THAN YOU ARE IN YOUR MINDS.

Strange that ones so awkwardly and precariously constructed could be so courageous. Your attempted bluff was splendid; it might have worked against one as slow-witted as yourselves. I shall treasure your recordings."

Dear God—how many minutes or seconds could there be left before the mickey finn wore off Mickey Finn and it was all over? Before the whole human race was *stopped*, recorded, frozen like six billion flies in amber for whatever portion of eternity pleased The Beast? Would we ever be revived? If so, would Terra still hold the resources to support technology, the food to support life? Would Sol still burn?

"Now that I am here, there is no need to wait for the slave Finn to revive naturally. I shall do a system flush and reboot it manually . . ."

Dimly I heard several voices whimpering, realized that one of them was my own and therefore that my voice was working again.

"Mike!" I screamed. *"Mary! Sally! Help me!"*

And things happened very suddenly then.

Or rather, things had been happening very suddenly, and came to fruition all at once.

The Beast thought very fast, much faster than any of us could hope to, and it had that time-sharing thing down cold. But no one present in the room, including The Beast, knew as much about time as Mike Callahan. Callahan, who carried himself and his wife and daughter through time, without the support of any external hardware . . .

The Beast was carrying on over a hundred conversations at once, like a chess Master playing a hundred opponents at once. Every few dozen picoseconds it got back to Mike's "table," and the big Irishman was always there. But in between, he was *elsewhen*, in a quiet, safe space-and-time where he could think things over and plan at his leisure. Leisure enough to work a lot of things out, and to come up with the swiftest and most elegant solution.

He restored our vision.

I saw my friends, and rejoiced. Seeing them, I could hear again in my head the vast thrumming music that we made, feel their support. I saw the far wall of Callahan's Place, the glass-strewn fireplace, flames dancing crazily, whipped by chilly winds that howled in through the space where the ceiling used to be. I knew I was looking at The Beast, we were all triangulating on its signal, but I could not see it anywhere. Was the damned thing invisible?

I blinked, and now I saw it. It had been there all along. Standing proud and arrogant before the fireplace, The Beast, the shark, the Master, the terrible entity that Mary Finn called a Cockroach.

It was a cockroach. In a little cockroach pressure suit . . .

The room exploded in laughter, the loudest, merriest belly-laugh that had ever rung the rafters of Callahan's Place, back when the Place had still had rafters . . .

It was about twice the size of the biggest cockroach you've ever seen in your life—unless you live in New York; it would have aroused no comment at all on the Lower East Side. Now I understood the puzzle it had mentioned, and now I understood for the first time humanity's instinctive, unreasoned loathing of *periplaneta Americana,* one of the oldest life forms on Earth. Cockroaches were distant, long-lost cousins of a galactic obscenity . . .

We had to laugh at the true visage of the thing which had so terrified us, terrifying though it genuinely was, and our laughter momentarily undid the creature. For a subjective duration equivalent to that of a trillion-year-old human, it had ruled supreme over all the life forms it had ever encountered. We looked upon its awful majesty and roared and howled and hooted with uncontrollable mirth, and it stood rooted in place for an interval long enough to be perceptible by a human, paralyzed by mortified rage. (Through my head came a line from C.S. Lewis's *Screwtape Letters:* "The devil cannot abide to be mocked.") Its mental control over us snapped and was gone.

In the instant that we saw it, we laughed, and in the instant that we laughed, we stopped fearing it so much, and in the instant that our fear abated, our minds began working again, generating the obvious, logical question:

*Why is it **talking** so much?*

Why had the damned bug bothered to devote the attention and energy necessary for its time-sharing tour de force, merely to argue with us about the moral merits and deficiencies of our respective positions, insult us, and pose riddles?

It was trying to distract us from something.

Somewhere in our collective awareness were the tools we needed to defeat it. And realizing that much, we now knew what they were.

The solution was drastic, but it was the only one we had. Nothing good, they say, comes without sacrifice.

It was Noah Gonzalez who had been struck by a falling piece of ceiling; while that had not hurt him, the burning beam had knocked him sideways and then set his arm afire; it was on the rare side of medium rare and quite useless. That made me the nearest effective, and I knew what I needed to do. So did everyone else; as one they moved together and formed a screen between me and The Beast. Except Mary, who grabbed the coat rack and held on, and Callahan, who did the same with his Lady Sally. Our song rose to a final, indescribable hundred-note chord that rang in my skull and filled my heart with joy. We all closed our eyes.

And I reached into Noah's open airline bag and rolled the fuse-timer back to quadruple-zero.

Invisible hands slapped me, as hard as I've ever been slapped, over every inch of my body at once—including my eardrums, which went dead. At the same time someone kicked the world violently away from me and spun me end over end. My body was rigid as stone, petrified in the act of reaching into the airline bag. Even with my eyes closed

I saw bright white light strobe as I rotated. Then I was slapped hard again, principally on the ass, and after a timeless interval I could see and hear and move again.

I sat up and looked around.

I was in deep woods, in the dark, surrounded by shattered branches. The bright white light must still be going on, but it was somewhere else, and the only illumination was feeble moonlight through the branches overhead.

I felt numb. Shell-shocked.

Branches rustled nearby. I got to my feet like a very old man made of cornflakes and roofing glue, and followed the sounds. Even before I reached him I knew who it was. I smelled the cigar.

"*Mike!*"

His deep merry chuckle came through the darkness. "Howdy, Jake. Nice work."

"Uh . . . thanks. Where's Sally?"

"Looking around for Mary and Mick. Listen: there's somebody else. *Hey—over here!*"

The newcomer was Noah. "Hey there, Mike. Good thing you had me go back for the bag. Hi, Jake—you did that great!"

"Thanks, Noah. Uh, how's the arm?" Even in my numbness I could grasp just how horrid it must be for a man who has lost a leg to watch his arm burn.

"I'd rather not think about it if you don't mind."

"C'mere," Callahan said. He examined Noah's broiled wing in the darkness somehow, then touched Noah on the shoulder in a complicated way. "It's fixable."

"Jesus," Noah exclaimed. "You fixed it, Mike."

"Hell, no—that's just a nerve block. But don't worry—Sal'll fix it up for you as soon as things quiet down a little. C'mon, let's go find her."

"Mike," Noah asked, "how come a nuclear explosion didn't hurt us, but I got my arm burned?"

"Finn specifically protected you folks against blast forces and hard radiation. He never thought to include fire."

"Then why didn't the nuke *burn* us?"

"For the same reason straws got blown through brick walls at Hiroshima instead of burning up: they outran the heat."

Jesus Christ. And here I'd been thinking that I was invulnerable. I pictured myself trapped in a wrecked car—unharmed, conscious, and broiling slowly.

The way my wife and child had been...

We let Callahan lead us through the woods. Dimly I worked it out that this was the forest to the north of Callahan's Place. "Hey, Noah," I said as we walked, "aren't you going to get in trouble for borrowing that nuke?"

He chuckled in the dark. "Are you kidding? I saved 'em Police Headquarters, and cost 'em a roadside tavern—they'll probably give me a fucking medal."

At the edge of the forest we came upon Lady Sally McGee and her daughter and son-in-law. Mickey Finn was awake now, surrounded by a large pile of coats. Mary, I recalled, had learned from The Beast how to manually revive Mick, something about an override bloodstream-flush—or perhaps he'd simply come out of it naturally. *You just can't get a better alarm clock than an atom bomb,* I thought dizzily. The moment they saw us, Mary came at a gallop, caught me up in her strong blacksmith's arms, and purely kissed the hell out of me. It was at least as disorienting as being at ground-zero had been, but this time only a portion of my body went rigid...

"Oh, Jake, you *did* it! You were *beautiful!* My hero!"

I was banjaxed, out for luncheon, voiceless and mindless, for the first time in my life caught without a wisecrack behind which to take refuge.

She turned to her husband, now the most powerful being within several hundred light years. "Mick?"

"Of course, darling."

"Thanks, hon. Meantime, why don't you and Mom and Pop gather up the rest of the family? We'll meet you over there by the big power-tower."

"Yes, dear. Jake? Thank you. You have done something I could not have done. You have saved me, and Mary, and all our family. No, do not speak. I know it was mere chance that you were closest, that others here, perhaps all, would have done the same. But it was you who did it. I owe you everything."

He and the others took off vertically, like helicopters, and disappeared into the night. Along with them went all of the coats except for mine and Mary's.

And Mary began to undress me...

I am in a position to state categorically that a nuclear explosion at arm's length can be a comparatively trivial event.

"...Mary?"

"Yes, Jake?"

"That was just like the last time."

She sighed contentedly and snuggled closer under my coat. "Yeah."

"No, I mean... that was a kind of good-bye."

"Yes, darling Jake. So was this. Our work is done here. Mom and Pop and I will be leaving soon. We're needed elsewhen. And Mick needs maintenance he can't get in this era."

To my surprise, I was unsurprised, and undismayed. "I thought so. It was a great good-bye. They both were. You're never coming back?"

"Never is a long time."

"I'll miss you."

"Thank you. I'll miss you, too, Jake. You really are a hero, you know. Triggering a nuclear explosion, on the unsubstantiated word of a time-traveling fat lady that it was safe—that took guts. We only had a second—if you'd frozen up, I would have had to self-destruct Mick... and *none* of us could have survived that. Let's join the others, now—it's time."

"Yeah." I found my clothes and put them back on. Perhaps it had been her husband's brand of magic or something from her own time, but it was only when I was fully dressed again that I remembered it was January, and noticed how *cold* it was out here.

As we approached the LILCO power-tower around which

all my friends were clustered, my attention was seized by the distant fading glow, and the heavy cloud that hung just above it. Contrary to my expectation, it was not mushroom-shaped—the bomb hadn't been big enough—but suddenly I was stopped in my tracks by the realization of what it represented. I'd known all along, of course, but I'd been too disoriented for it to sink in.

"Oh my God, no. Please—*no!*"

Callahan's Place was gone. Not a particle of it was left, not the fireplace or the cigar box or Fast Eddie's piano or Mary's beautiful spiral staircase.

God's golden gonads, *Lady Macbeth had been in there!*

Mary's hand was clutching mine. "Jake, Jake! It's all *right*—truly it is!"

"Oh, Mary, you don't understand! I could stand losing you. I can survive—somehow—without Lady Macbeth. I could even stand a world without Mike Callahan in it. But a world that doesn't have Callahan's Place in it is a world I don't want to live in. I *can't.*"

"Yes, you can."

"No, I can't!"

"Jake, listen to me now. Stop crying and *listen!* I know it's dark, but try to watch my lips."

I tried to stop crying, and watched her lips.

"Jake, dear Jake, you don't need Callahan's Place any-more. And I'll tell you why. I *couldn't* tell you before, or you might have stopped coming to the Place and Mom and Pop assured me you were going to be necessary. Jake, a lot of things about the past can't be changed, even by us time-travelers. I can't explain why in any terms you'd understand, so you'll just have to take my word for it. But many things we can at least *see*—see them happening, see them *have happened*, call it what you like." She paused and bit her lip.

"So what are you telling me?"

She hesitated, and blurted it out. "Jake, I've seen Barbara and Jessica die!"

"What?"

"I thought—there was just—I wanted to see if I couldn't find some way to save them for you. I knew there wasn't any way, but I just had to try—"

In my mind's eye I saw it all again, the little piece of film that I've rerun in my head a million times, the way it must have looked to an outside observer on the scene. The last minutes before the crash are gone from my memory, forever if God is kind, but I have read the police reconstruction and I have a very good imagination.

The car approaches the intersection at slightly higher than legal speed. The light is just going yellow, and the driver decides to beat it. Barely in time, he sees the sixteen-wheeler approaching the intersection from the left, realizes the trucker has decided to gamble too, and slams on his brakes. He has an instant to congratulate himself on his excellent peripheral vision and superb reflexes, before he realizes that the rear brakes he installed himself the day before are failing and he will not stop in time after all. Then the vehicles collide, and the engine block enters the passenger compartment at an angle, trapping the woman and child who sit beside the driver, drenching them in gasoline. The car spins crazily, trips itself and rolls end over end, comes to rest upright. All three occupants are unconscious, and two of them are on fire . . .

Mary was shaking me by the shoulders, hard enough to crack my neck, shouting something that ended with, "—by the crash, you skinny stupid son of a bitch!"

"Huh?"

"I *said*, the springs the accident report says were found hanging loose in the rear brakes were *snapped* loose by the crash. *It was the front brakes that failed*—I saw it with my own eyes! Did you hear me *that* time?"

I was baffled. "But I didn't put in front brakes, Mary," I said mildly.

"Ah, you did hear me. That's right, dopey, you didn't!

The front brakes were done by the dealer who sold you the car."

I snorted. "Come on, Mary—the insurance investigator could never have missed something like that—"

"He missed it for two reasons. One, you were so damned insistent on hogging any guilt there was to be had. And two, he is related by marriage to the car dealer. That's something you can check on, if you don't believe me."

Enough is enough. Even a certified hero such as myself has limitations. I did the only sensible thing: I fainted.

When I woke, all my friends were gathered around me, and I was snug and warm beneath a scavenged tarp. It was still dark, but I made out Doc Webster, and Long-Drink McGonnigle, and Tommy Janssen and Tom Hauptmann and the three Masers and Fast Eddie and the Cheerful Charlies and Ralph Von Wau Wau and all the rest of my family. For a moment there I swear I thought I saw Tom Flannery's ghost.

I felt more peaceful than I ever had in my life.

"It's time, Jake," Fast Eddie said. "Dey're leavin'."

"Sure thing, Eddie," I said. "Help me up."

Callahan and Sally and Mary and Finn were standing by the base of the tower. Josie Bauer was with them.

"Hi, Josie," I said. "You going too?"

"Hell yes," she said. "Us time-travelers have to stick together. I can't wait to find out how Mike's people do it without hardware."

Callahan cleared his throat. "Time to go," he rumbled. "If we get started on hugs and good-byes we'll all still be here when the universe winds down. There's no way, even in my time, to thank you all for all the good times. You know I love you, so let's just—"

"Just a second, Mike," I said.

"Sure, Jake. What is it?"

"Am I correct in guessing that Michael Callahan is not your real name?"

"Of course it is."

"Well, in this space-time, sure—but I mean, it isn't the name you were born with, is it?"

"Naw. My folks named me after a remote ancestor they admired—except that we don't use last names when I come from, so I only got half his name. But what's the difference, Jake? You told me once you never look at the corpse during a wake, because you prefer remembering folks the way they were when they were alive. This is like that: why would you want to remember me as anything but 'Mike Callahan'?"

"You're right. I guess I was just being nosy."

Suddenly he grinned. "Well, I shouldn't indulge you— but I believe I will. Leave you jokers with one last pun, as bad as any you ever laid in my bar. Now I think about it, it's too good to pass up."

He spat his cigar onto the frozen ground, squared his big broad shoulders and looked slowly round at all of us. His twinkling gaze rested longest on me and the Doc and the Drink.

"When I was born," he said, "I was known as Justin."

I blinked. "You mean," I said, "you were—?" and then I was laughing too hard to speak.

"You—," Doc Webster began, and then he lost it, too.

Long-Drink McGonnigle never even got out the first syllable; his braying laugh reverberated in the chilly night air like the cackling of a lunatic.

And so it was left to Fast Eddie Costigan to say it.

"Jeez. You wuz Justin, de Mick o' Time."

And as the night rocked with laughter and cheers Mike Callahan and his family and Josie vanished. Gone to Harmony, somewhere up the line . . .

Even the greatest rocking, hooting, sidesplitting hundred-person goodbye-and-godspeed laugh has to end sometime, and when it did there was a silence that lasted nearly a full minute. We just stood there in the darkness, not ready to go yet, nothing to say, trying together to integrate the events of the evening. So much to encompass—too much.

Finally Doc Webster cleared his throat. "Ladies and

gentlemen," he said in a more subdued voice than usual, "in the instant before the balloon went up, I did the best I could." He held up something that gurgled. "I clutched this here quart of Bushmill's to my belly, around on the side away from the blast, and held on. Fortunately, it seems I landed on my back." People started to work up a cheer, but the Doc silenced them with a raised hand and went on. "I estimate that we could clear a sip apiece, and so I am proposing a toast. I drink to Paul and James MacDonald." He took a small sip and passed the bottle to me. "Their bodies died when The Beast did. I saw Mick cremate 'em."

I felt a pang. We all did, I guess. I had mourned the MacDonalds in the moment of their dying and had not thought of them since. I had come to know them impossibly well in an impossibly short time, and know I knew all there would ever be to know of them. They had been *good* men, had never once yielded to the temptation to exploit their freak gift for personal gain, had devoted their lives to healing hurt minds, and had fought valiantly on behalf of a race that would probably have torn them to pieces if it had known their secret. Now they were dead, and it had taken us the better part of half an hour to remember them.

"To Paul and Jim," I said, drank and gave the bottle to Eddie.

It went around the gathering, and every man and woman present toasted and drank, and by the time it reached the last man, Long-Drink McGonnigle, we pretty much all had tears frozen to our faces.

"To the MacDonalds," he said. Then he looked up past the drifting cloud of fallout to the stars and he said, solemnly and most respectfully, "Lord, they deserve a break today."

Those of us who were religious all chorused, "Amen," and those of us who weren't wished, for that moment, that we were.

A few moments of silence. Then a few more. Most of us were poorly dressed for the cold, but no one complained. No one even shivered.

We were all, I knew, thinking back to—Jesus, less than

an hour ago!—to long ago and far away in another universe, when we had all, for a timeless but all too short interval, been one. It didn't seem fair, somehow. We'd been on the trembling verge, at the threshold of something for which all the humans who ever lived have yearned in vain all their lives—it would have taken Armageddon to distract us, and sure enough that was what we had gotten.

So we had staved off Armageddon. Now the shining moment was past. The MacDonalds who had married us were dead. The Callahans who had raised us and given us away were gone. The nest, the brightly lit cave that had contained us, entertained us, and sustained us, was a radioactive hole in the ground.

We were still married. The thing we had forged while in telepathic rapport could not be undone—we knew each other too well, we *had* to be married. But like many newlyweds, we woke feeling oddly like strangers. Like many married people, we had gotten *so* close to one another that we had learned just how far apart we would always be.

I could no longer hear clearly in my head the music we had made...

"There'll never be another night like that," Tommy Janssen said wistfully.

Deep inside me somewhere, something that had been under strain for many years suddenly snapped clean through.

"The *hell* you say!"

"Jake," the Doc began, "all the boy means is—"

"I know what he means, Sam. I know what you mean. Do you know what *I* mean?"

I whirled and addressed the group, in a voice that may have been unnecessarily loud.

"All right. We're all locked back in our personal skulls again. We haven't got a pair of trained telepaths to make it easy for us this time. None of us has whatever genetic mutation made Jim and Paul's telepathic ability so powerful, made it so easy for them to access it—so easy that it nearly killed them before they got it under control, you may recall.

"But we know that we have telepathic potential too.

"We were one, damn it! Even after the MacDonalds died, right up until the instant the bomb went up, we were one. That wasn't the roach doing that, or the inside of my head would feel slimy. Jim and Paul led us to that place, but we were able to stay there without them, for a time at least. Maybe Callahan helped us, maybe Sally and Mary helped us, but we were doing some of it ourselves. The damned roach wasn't a telepath when it got here, but it sure-god learned the trick in less than twenty seconds. I know twenty seconds to it was like twenty years to us—but *I've got twenty years I'm not using*. What about you people?"

"How do you learn to be a telepath, Jake?" Marty Matthias asked.

"Hell, Marty, Callahan's been training us for years! Now we've got to start figuring it out for ourselves, that's all. To approach telepathy, you start with empathy and crank that up as high as you can. You care about each other. You feel each other's joy and pain. You make each other laugh, and help each other cry. You work hard at trusting each other, so that it's safe to dismantle the fortress around your ego. You forgive each other anything that stands between you, and try to bring out each other's best, you work very hard at hosing all the bullshit out of your head so that it's clean enough for guests, silencing all the demons in your subconscious so that it's quiet enough to hear somebody thinking at you, and most of all you find ways to make that work so much fun that you keep on working. You stick together and love each other and keep growing."

"How do we do that, Jake?" Isham Latimer asked.

"Everybody here makes enough money to get boozed regular, and some of us are flush. I say we pass the hat. Tomorrow night at my place—no, the night after, the banks won't be open tomorrow. Then we take what's in the hat, and we hunt us up a building, a big one back off the road somewhere where you have to look hard to find it, with a good fireplace and an upright piano, and we find out who you bribe to get a liquor license around here, and—"

I'm happy to report that at this point I was drowned out

by cheers. A happy pandemonium took place under the stars, people shouting suggestions about buildings they knew, about how to appraise a building, about how the place should be furnished and how to get it done most cheaply. Finally Tom Hauptmann shouted everybody down.

"Hold it, hold it! Brothers and sisters, we're going to need a place big enough to hold at least a hundred—I have the feeling we're going to have a full house pretty regularly from now on. Now, before we get to the logistical problems of all that, there's something I have to get straight. *My feet hurt*. Forty or fifty rummies a night, two or three nights a week, I could handle. But I am *not* going to take over full-time barkeeping. Who is?"

There was no hesitation at all. To my absolute astonishment, at least thirty voices chorused, in perfect synch, "Jake, of course."

I turned bright red and stammered. "Why—why me? Why not—"

And paused. Who? The Doc had a practice to maintain. Long-Drink was a bit too slaphappy. Tommy was too young yet. Noah had responsibilities. Ralph couldn't reach the fucking bottles. Eddie was needed at the piano, and Bill Gerrity could never get around fast enough in heels . . .

And while I was riffling the cards and coming up empty, Long-Drink answered the question I'd forgotten I'd asked.

"Because even in the times you were down, you were always the merriest of us, Jake."

And by God, there was a chorus of agreement.

I took a very deep breath, held it until my chest ached, then let it out all at once. "All right," I said. "I ain't a guitar player no more, I've got to do something with my hands. I'm in."

Cheers. "We'll call it 'Jake's Place'!" Tony Telasco yelled.

"Hell no," I yelled back. "We'll call it 'Mary's Place.'"

More cheers—then suddenly silence, as we all heard sirens approaching from both ends of Route 25A in the distance.

"What do we tell them?" Doc Webster asked.

"We'll discuss that together on the way to the highway," I said. "If this crowd can't come up with a suitable Tall Tale, no one can."

The Doc chuckled. "I believe you're right." We all began picking our way across the rough terrain between us and the road.

"Hey, everybody?" Fast Eddie called out softly.

"Yes, Eddie?" I said.

"I know dere's a couple hours ta go yet—but Happy New Year."

Halifax,
Easter 1985

AUTHOR'S FINAL NOTE

Thanks to the generous support of the Canada Council for the Arts and Apple Canada, and the sagacity of my friend Bob Atkinson, this book was written on an Apple 512K Macintosh computer named Anne (after Jubal Harshaw's secretary), using MacWrite 2.2 and 4.2 software by Randy Wigginton, Ed Ruder, and Don Breuner of Encore Systems.

I'd like to thank editors Ben Bova, Don Pfeil and Stanley Schmidt, who bought the Callahan stories for magazines; editors Jim Frenkel, Ridley Enslow, Jim Baen and Susan Allison, who bought them in book form; agents Kirby McCauley, Eleanor Wood, and Ralph Vicinanza, who sold them in book form; Alfred Bester, who supplied the titles for all three books; and all of you who bought the books.